PASSION FRUIT

Also by Daniel Pennac in English translation

Fiction

THE FAIRY GUNMOTHER

THE SCAPEGOAT

WRITE TO KILL

Essay

READS LIKE A NOVEL

Daniel Pennac

PASSION FRUIT

Translated from the French by
Ian Monk

THE HARVILL PRESS
LONDON

First published with the title *Aux fruits de la passion*
by Editions Gallimard, 1999

First published in Great Britain in 2001 by
The Harvill Press
2 Aztec Row
Berners Road
London N1 0PW

www.harvill.com

1 3 5 7 9 8 6 4 2

© Editions Gallimard, 1999
English translation © Ian Monk, 2001

Daniel Pennac asserts the moral right to be
identified as the author of this work

A CIP catalogue record for this book
is available from the British Library

This translation is published with the financial
assistance of the French Ministry of Culture

ISBN 1 86046 747 4 (hbk)
ISBN 1 86046 801 2 (pbk)

Designed and typeset in Minion at
Libanus Press, Marlborough, Wiltshire

Printed and bound in Great Britain by Clays Ltd, St Ives plc

The Random House Group Limited supports The Forest Stewardship
Council® (FSC®), the leading international forest-certification organisation.
Our books carrying the FSC label are printed on FSC®-certified paper.
FSC is the only forest-certification scheme supported by the leading
environmental organisations, including Greenpeace. Our
paper procurement policy can be found at
www.randomhouse.co.uk/environment

MIX
Paper | Supporting
responsible forestry
FSC® C018179

For Tonino

A big sloppy kiss: fifteen dead
CHRISTIAN MOUNIER

I

*In which we learn that Thérèse is in love
and with whom*

Chapter 1

WE SHOULD LIVE in hindsight. We decide things too quickly. I should never have invited that character to dinner. It was a hasty surrender with disastrous consequences. True, I was under enormous pressure. The whole tribe was on my case, trying to convince me in their various ways. It was carpet bombing:

"What do you mean?" Jeremy yelled. "Thérèse's got herself a bloke and you don't even want to meet him?"

"I never said that."

Louna chipped in:

"Thérèse's found a gentleman who's interested in her, which is about as likely as discovering tulips on Mars, and you couldn't care less?"

"I never said that I couldn't care less."

"You're not even a tad curious, Benjamin?"

That was Clara with her voice of velvet.

"Do you even know what Thérèse's boyfriend does for a living?" Half Pint asked from behind his rose-tinted glasses.

No, I didn't even know what he did for a living.

"Books!"

"Books?"

"That's what Thérèse said. She says he does books for a living."

Forbidding access to our hardware shop to a man who does books for a living was like wiping out Half Pint's entire system of values. From my own good self to Loussa de Casamance, passing by our friend Theo, old Risson, Clément Clément, Thian, Yasmina or Cissou the Snow, everyone he'd ever known was into storytelling.

"Is that right?" I asked Julie later. "Is this Thérèsophile really a writer?"

"Whether he's a writer or a garage mechanic, you're going to have to accept the situation," she replied. "So why don't you give in at once and organise a dinner party?"

As for Mum, she was off living her love life somewhere else as usual. She was told the glad tidings over the phone one morning at about ten – over discreet crunchings of toast, she was probably calling us while breakfasting in bed. She then said what she always says when one of her daughters becomes besotted.

"Thérèse is in love? But that's mar-vell-ous! I only hope she'll be as happy as I am."

Then she hung up.

As this was women's business, there was no point trying to get male help. But I still consulted my mates. Hadouch, Mo and Simon were all of the same mind:

"You've never liked it when your sisters get laid, Ben. You want to keep them all for yourself. It's your 'Mediterranean mentality' as you Whites put it."

As for Old Amar, he was quietly fatalistic:

"*Inch Allah*, my son. What woman wants, God wants. Yasmina wanted me because God willed that I wanted Yasmina. Understand? Your mind must be as broad as Allah's heart."

4

I thought about Stojil. What advice would old Stojil have given me while leaning over our chessboard, if he hadn't died before his time? Probably the same as when Julie got it into her belly to procreate:

"Leave it to Thérèse."

An answer that was quite close to Rabbi Razon's laconic ontology:

"The human race is a woman's decision, Benjamin. Even Hitler couldn't do anything to stop that."

This was then confirmed by Gervaise, my son's second mother, Julie's stand-in, a holy soul who has devoted her life to the redemption of streetwalkers. I went up to see her in the playgroup she'd opened by Rue des Abbesses for the entire neighbourhood's whoresons and daughters. That illegitimate offspring gambolled around her in an odour of milk and virgin flesh. Above that seething mass, Gervaise rose up like a rock of motherhood.

"If Thérèse wants to have a baby, Benjamin, then she will. It's a question of appetite. Even prossies can't resist it. Just look around yourself."

She gestured above the whorelets who were clambering up onto her lap.

"If I can't stop this happening, then how can you?"

She had ironically called her playgroup *Passion Fruit*. Clara had a job there, arriving each morning with Verdun, What An Angel and Monsieur Malaussène. After all, they were all passion fruit. And so Gervaise and Clara sweetly presided over their little bordello.

As for Theo, my old mate, the man who prefers men, he treated me to a series of lamentations one evening when he was down in the dumps:

"What do you want, in the end? For Thérèse to start dating other girls? In homosexuality, there's a *sameness factor* that winds up getting depressing. Believe you me, it's something I've looked into, Ben."

"What's more," he then added, "Thérèse's been to see me. You haven't got much room for manoeuvre."

"What did she tell you?"

"What she'd like to be able to tell you. But she's scared of you, because you're the big bro. I'm just the old Queen Mother who gets told everything and repeats nothing."

Then, of course, my work at the Vendetta Press started to suffer. And there was nothing to be hoped for from Queen Zabo:

"Piss me off once more with your family, Malaussène, and I'll show you the door. And for good."

I didn't take that too well.

"OK, your Majesty, I'm fired."

When the door had slammed, I heard her yell out after me:

"And don't count on any golden handshakes!"

In the corridor, my old friend Loussa de Casamance, the Senegalese expert in Chinese literature, asked me:

"*Chengfa, haizi?*" (Been punished again, kid?)

All I said was that, this time, I was definitely going for good.

"*Wo gai zou le, yilaoyongyi!*"

"The verb comes at the end, kid. How many times do I have to tell you! *Yilaoyongyi, wo gai zou le!*"

With a family and friends like that, I was once more alone with a problem that wasn't mine. So Thérèse Malaussène was in love, was she? My brittle Thérèse! My Murano crystal spirit. So fragile ... and in love! In tribal memory, love had never fostered anything but the irreparable in this family! Mum, Clara and

6

Louna certainly knew all about that. How many break-ups, how many failed relationships, how many violent deaths and how many orphans were we going to end up with? Love had paved our family with corpses, which had an exponential quantity of kids frolicking above them, and yet these women were ready to start all over? With fresh heart to delight at that rosy flush on Thérèse's hollow cheeks, which was instantly identifiable as love's mark, while I'd been hoping it was just a case of tuberculosis?

It's true. Take it as you like it, but I'd pinned all my hopes on Koch's bacillus. There could be just one explanation for that pinkness on my wan and ghastly Thérèse, that strange sentimentality in her dry speech, that glowing aura around her cold body, those feverish daydreams, her glowing eyes: she had consumption. You could catch TB just by being a romantic, which Thérèse certainly was. Six months of antibiotics and we'd hear no more of the matter.

I kept up that illusion as long as I could. Then, one evening, I decided to get things straight. Half an hour after lights out, I went into the kids' room and leant over Thérèse's bed:

"Are you asleep Thérèse, my darling?"

She was staring into the night.

"Thérèse, what's the matter?"

She said:

"I love."

I tried an easy exit:

"What do you love?"

But she wasn't having any:

"I love a man."

After a pregnant pause, she added:

"I want you all to meet him."

And, as I remained silent:

7

"Whenever you want, Benjamin."

So that's what they'd been up to for the last three days. Wearing down my resistance. A war of attrition. I was defending my last positions and knew I was beaten. Finally, it was Julius the Dog that won the day.

"What about you, what do you reckon?"

He raised his uncontradictable eyes at me.

"OK, we'll invite him round tomorrow evening."

Julius the Dog also liked storytellers.

Chapter 2

H E DID DO books, but he didn't write them. He audited them. He was a Councillor at the National Audit Office. Half Pint was still at an age when there is hope in ambiguities. He heard what he wanted to hear. But this character was an auditor in a three-piece suit without the slightest grain of fiction in his being. Thérèse introduced us:

"Marie-Colbert de Roberval," she said. "He's a Councillor with the Audit Office. A Councillor Grade One," she added in her sweetest tones.

Julius the Dog immediately clamped his snout into Marie-Colbert's butt and then stared up at me in horror. Our financially bookish lover was odourless.

"How do you do?" said I.

"His brother hanged himself," Thérèse announced.

I don't know if it was the news itself, its unexpected nature or Thérèse's unruffled tone, but our tribe's reactions lacked any true hint of compassion.

"Jesus!" Theo muttered.

"You're kidding!" said Jeremy.

"What with?" Half Pint asked.

"Sorry," Louna murmured, so vaguely that it was impossible to say if she was commiserating with the dead, comforting the quick, or presenting our apologies.

Clara photographed the couple. Her flash broke the ice a bit, and Thérèse pointed round at us while the Polaroid was spitting out its snap.

"My family," she said.

No doubt about it. She had that smile of a girl in love who's introducing her lover to his loving soon-to-be in-laws.

"Clara photographs everything," she added with a giggle.

"I am delighted to meet you all at last," Marie-Colbert proclaimed.

His voice lacked character but not intent; he'd wrapped it all up in that final "at last".

Right now, I don't really know what to say about that dinner party. Thérèse had insisted on the entire tribe being there: Theo in the role of our absent mother, Amar as the father we'd never had, Julie as a legitimate spouse, Gervaise as our moral guarantor; Old Sole appeared as a deserving retired artisan grandfather, Hadouch, Simon and Mo as provincial cousins, and Loussa de Casamance as a cultivated uncle, in case the conversation hit intellectual heights. Clara had done her best cordon bleu routine, Jeremy asked Thérèse "if he handed out Council houses" and Marie-Colbert had replied in his neutral tone that the sort of council he was on was quite different, Sole flaunted his City of Paris medal and hinted that he wouldn't be averse to accepting the Labour Medal as well, Louna grinned apologetically, Gervaise politely asked what the Audit Office audited exactly, Marie-Colbert then came out with a rapid briefing, from which it emerged that the above-mentioned Office policed the police of the Civil

Service and audited the stationery that their fellows in the old-boy network had rifled, Half Pint reckoned that he "was a natural storyteller", but most of this passed me by, occupied as I was trying to absorb my indigestible first impression.

Marie-Colbert was so tall, straight and well brought up that the tail of his jacket would never fail to bounce up neatly over his well-rounded buttocks. Hairless, fleshy and interestingly pale, he looked at the world with what was supposed to be an eagle eye. His handshake was firm – sport, like the rest of it, must have been part of his upbringing – and he came across as a music-lover, the sort who plays Bach at a predetermined hour of the day with metronomic precision. His sleeves looked a tad too short and it was impossible to say if he was balding or well-groomed.

Later that night, I woke Julie up to ask her what she thought of him.

"Nothing," she answered. "He's your typical fast-laner, that's all."

And that was precisely what bothered me. Where the hell had Thérèse picked up such a paragon of normality?

"At work," she replied when I asked her. "You know I never go out!"

Thérèse's work was fortune telling. She told it in a tiny Bohemian caravan which Hadouch, Mo and Simon had unearthed God alone knows where and deposited on four breeze blocks on Boulevard de Ménilmontant, just by the wall of Père-Lachaise cemetery, at the end of the market. Come rain, shine or snow storm, the entire human race queued up outside Thérèse's caravan. No matter how hard I tried, I just couldn't picture Marie-Colbert's head jutting up above that throng.

On the other hand, Thérèse never lied.

"All sorts of people consult me, you know. There's more to Paris than just Belleville!"

True enough. But to return to that dinner party, I reckon I know what really put me out. It was the Polaroid Clara took of the couple. She put it down on the tablecloth next to me, then went to fetch the plates from the kitchen and forgot it there. I've never really been into Polaroids . . . that grey slowly crystallising cloud . . . those faces looming up from a shallow pit . . . that spontaneous generation of an image . . . that unstoppable incarnation . . . and then that wonderful commemoration of a present time already in the past . . . no, there's a chemical mystery in all that which puts the fear of some primitive god in me . . . the fear of revelation maybe, of what will appear when everything has been revealed. So, I reckon I spent that wretched dinner party watching Thérèse and Marie-Colbert emerge into that square of hazy gelatine. And didn't our happy couple take their time about it! Thérèse appeared first. Thérèse with her angles. Like the first pencil strokes of a sketch. A bony, yellow Thérèse emerged with that consumptive blush on the cheeks of her still-nonexistent face . . . the crooked slit of her smile – she'd put on some lipstick for the first time in her life – . . . But who was she smiling at? There wasn't the slightest trace of Marie-Colbert. Thérèse filled out alone in a gap containing the first emerging pieces of furniture. Still no Marie-Colbert. Was I really scared? Did I really say to myself that Thérèse had hitched up with a vampire, who'd slipped out of Père-Lachaise cemetery to queue up outside her caravan and then bleed her dry? If I judge by the relief I felt when the Councillor Grade One finally loomed up, then such thoughts definitely had crossed my mind . . . his lovely suit came first . . . then him in his suit . . . and finally his face with my sister Thérèse smiling at it.

12

The entire meal must have drifted by, because the next thing I can remember about the evening was Marie-Colbert's broad face leaning over me, with its dull smile, piercing eyes, and the words he whispered to me while the tribe was going ecstatic over the snap.

"There are things we must discuss, Benjamin."

They all thought it was a really good likeness.

"Alone," he added.

And that the colours had come out great.

"Tomorrow at two pm."

What an absolutely charming couple!

"Would the bar at the Hotel Crillon suit you?"

A golden future.

"It's about the wedding."

II

In which we get to know Thérèse's fiancé better
What we think of him

Chapter 3

THE NEXT DAY, at the stroke of two in the gilt of the Crillon, Marie-Colbert de Roberval ("Call me MC2, Benjamin, that's what my fellows used to do at school"), aka MC2 told me of his intention to wed Thérèse as rapidly as possible. His professional ties did not leave him much time to haggle. He wasn't requesting my sister's hand. He was quite simply annexing it. He'd marry Thérèse in a fortnight's time, and there was an end to it.

"At Saint-Philippe-du-Roule."

"It will be a joint-estate marriage," MC2 went on, while stirring his coffee. "Everything I possess shall be hers. As for Thérèse . . ."

The silver spoons went pregnantly silent.

"She will be ample recompense."

All this to make me understand that Prince Charming was accepting my Cinderella with or without the carriage. (Aren't the moneyed diplomatic when they state the price of their feelings!)

"But do not conclude from this that Thérèse will live as a kept woman, Benjamin. That is not her style."

Silence. Deep stare. Weighing of words.

"Your sister is an extraordinary woman."

It was the first time Julius and I had heard anyone talk about

Thérèse in terms of womanhood. To return the favour, Julius affectionately plunged his dribbling snout into my future brother-in-law's crotch, while his tail gleefully swept away our half-empty cups. There was a shower of coffee, sugar bowls, a waiterly dance with napkins and sponges, down Julius, there's a good boy! Fresh biscuits, steaming coffee, immaculate doilies, and off we went again, please pardon my dog . . .

"Thérèse will continue working. She will quite simply move in a circle that is more . . ."

What adjective was he after? "Refined"? "Respectable"? "Lucrative"? "Informed"? "Powerful"? He abruptly sidetracked.

"Has she told you how we met?"

They met because of a hanged man. Marie-Colbert de Roberval (MC2)'s brother, Charles-Henri de Roberval (CH2), being the hanged man in question. And this hanging being a sad case of professional ethics. Here's what happened: MC2 went overboard a bit auditing the administrative budget of a ministry his brother had run a few years back, and CH2 hanged himself. Had Charles-Henri felt under suspicion, about to be called in to help the police with their inquiries? Was he afraid of seeing his name splashed across the papers?

"His worries were all the more absurd given that it was a routine investigation, and I can assure you that Charles-Henri's management had been irreproachable."

But for members of the de Roberval family, honour was their middle name, and public service a sacred duty. This had been the case since the days of Colbert himself! Despite having been raised to the aristocracy under Louis XIV, after the French Revolution they at once started serving the Republic.

"Two centuries of incorruptible Jacobinism, Benjamin, though

18

I must admit with slight right-wing leanings. I am sure that we do not vote the same way. But the main point is centralism, our shared heritage from the age of Louis XIV and the Revolution, wouldn't you agree?"

Anyway, Charles-Henri hanged himself. In the de Robervals' town house at 60 Rue Quincampoix, practically right in front of his brother's nose. Had he really done so because of Marie-Colbert's investigations? MC2 stopped sleeping, drinking and eating. He'd lost his appetite for life.

"That is the very word. Thérèse gave me back my appetite for life!"

All of which still didn't explain how they met.

"Through an old school chum. Another former minister."

Who'd met her through?

"His Chinese servant. Or Cantonese, to be precise. A poor swine from your neighbourhood whose wife had left him and who was having doubts about his virility. Your sister gave him an *I Ching* reading and sorted the whole thing out. The lost wife promptly returned to be impregnated."

"An *I Ching* reading?"

"A form of Chinese fortune telling using pieces of wood that form ideograms. A sort of spiritual pick-up-sticks, if you will."

"Did Thérèse do you an *I Ching* reading as well?"

No, she didn't. Following his old school chum's advice, Marie-Colbert went to consult Thérèse with Charles-Henri's date, time and place of birth, as though he were examining the future of a brother that was still very much alive. Thérèse had glanced at the data, then stared up at Marie-Colbert: "This man hanged himself a fortnight ago. He was your brother and you're wondering if it was all your fault. You're devastated."

"Those were her very words, Benjamin."

And those very words were confirmed by Thérèse that evening.

"It's true, Marie-Colbert could never have stopped Charles-Henri from killing himself. I've never seen such an awful horoscope. Just imagine it, Benjamin, Mars and Uranus in the 8th House! And, what's more, they were in opposition to Saturn! No, there really were too many conjunctions. I had a terrible time trying to reassure Marie-Colbert. He felt so terribly guilty. He so needed comforting . . . You know what, Benjamin, he really reminds me of you . . . So rational, and yet so emotive! So you saw him? How did it go? I'm all ears!"

All this at the family table, with the others of course lapping up every word.

"Where did you meet?" Clara asked.

"In the bar at the Crillon."

"Naff," Jeremy butted in. "Everything happens at the Hemingway Bar these days."

"How do you know that?" Half Pint asked.

"Shut it," Jeremy suggested.

"Shut it yourself," Half Pint advised.

"I'd say it was the Café Coste," proclaimed Theo, who had dropped in for dinner. "The Café Coste is where it's at now."

"The Hemingway Bar," Jeremy insisted. "The Hemingway Bar at the Ritz."

"The Café Coste," Theo repeated. "I swear to you. For the last six months it's been the Coste."

"Bullshit," Jeremy went.

"It all depends what you want to do," Clara intervened. "For example, if you're a photographer . . ."

"All the same, meeting up at the Crillon . . ." Louna whistled.

"Old hat," Jeremy concluded.

"What did he tell you?" Thérèse asked. "What did you talk about?"

"About your future, my lovely. And that of the nation."

That's right. MC2 had been firing on all cylinders. Thérèse's fortune-telling abilities had "literally amazed" him. With his flat intonation and large, lifeless body, he nevertheless reached the peak of effervescence. According to him, the future of the entire country depended on Thérèse. She incarnated "that intuition which is indispensable to any government, and a necessary corrective to blind rationality". She was the Republic's "right hemisphere", "that intuitive part of the mind that has so foolishly been overlooked by our educational system, which rather favours a rationality that constantly comes up against its own limitations".

I swear it. He really did speak like that. Right off the cuff. He smiled haughtily:

"And you can believe what I am telling you, Benjamin – I, Marie-Colbert de Roberval, whose first name rings with authority and whose surname commands respect."

(I did tell you he was a nifty speaker . . .) Getting carried away, he ordered a couple of cognacs.

"Well, it certainly altered my outlook, old chap! The ten minutes I spent with your sister were sufficient for me to allot the soul its true importance. And let no-one accuse me of being superstitious!"

On the contrary, by marrying Thérèse, Marie-Colbert was intending to chase away all the fortune tellers that haunted the corridors of power. Thérèse was the real McCoy.

"With Thérèse, we would never have dissolved!"

"Dissolved?"

"Dissolved parliament! Last year. You do remember! The deputies . . . and the lost election. If we had consulted Thérèse, we would never have gone to the polls early. We would still be in command, and France would be all the better for it."

Of course, of course.

"And if my brother had met you, he would never have hanged himself."

Sorry?

He fell silent. The cognac was rotating between his palms. It was as if he was trying to divine that dead man's future in it. I took the opportunity to summon up a vision in my own glass: Thérèse dropping the coffee grounds and reading the future in VSOP . . . my Thérèse swapping her tarot cards for a bridge evening . . . I saw her there clearly in the belly of my glass, Thérèse bent down over the beige of a bridge drive, reading high society fortunes in the dummy hand laid out in front of her. It was my first flash. Oh, nothing really special, just a fleeting premonition, brief but clear as a decree: I was in the shit. That's it. This wedding was going to drop me, Benjamin Malaussène, personally in the shit. And not just any old pile of shit, not one of those common-or-garden compost heaps that fate had flung me in until then, no this was a sewer of oceanic dimensions, compared to which everything I'd already experienced was going to be peanuts. I didn't know what I was going to be accused of exactly, but, down in the bottom of my cognac and in the velvet silence of that bar, things were looking blacker and blacker. This time, I was really going to cop it. With no way out. I wasn't going to be accused of this or that, no. This time I was going to be accused of *everything*.

As though echoing my terror, Marie-Colbert (Marie-Colbert!) distinctly said:

"And your job as a scapegoat, Benjamin . . ."

No doubt about it, a copro-nimbus was gathering over my head.

"If you had only taught the rudiments of scapegoatery to my brother, then he would still be alive and well today."

What's the time? Time I was off, for sure. MC2 went on, staring into my eyes, as though confiding in someone for the first time in his life.

"Like me, Charles-Henri was a pure product of our alma mater, that is to say a scapegoat, like you. The only difference is that we are ignorant of that fact. *L'Ecole Nationale d'Administration* prepares us for the highest posts, we are good students when we begin and potential ministers when we leave. But what is a minister, Benjamin? Or a Permanent Secretary? Or an administrator? Or the head of a chain? They are fuses, my dear fellow! Goats that are massacred at each political turnaround. We think we have been trained to serve and we are in fact destined for the chopping block! A professor of scapegoatery, that's what our school is lacking! Someone of your stamp, who could prepare the elite for sacrifice, while they imagine they are being primed for power. I can assure you that our school needs you!"

I should have felt honoured. Someone wanted to take me on just after Queen Zabo had fired me. And the School of Schools with it! I could be teaching the cream of the cream! But, God knows why, instead of a laurel garland, it felt as though that cloud of shit had settled on my head.

"Even if he had been guilty, Charles-Henri would never have hanged himself if you had been his teacher! As he was an excellent student, he would have played out his part as a scapegoat, and so would have survived."

The cloud was already starting to reek enough to make even

23

Julius the Dog smell of roses. Why me? Why was it always me?

"I am not joking, Benjamin. The doors of our school are open to you. One word from you, and I shall speak to those responsible."

No, no! Very nice of you, but not a word to those responsible, definitely not! I had to be off, I had an appointment somewhere, that's what, it had all been very nice . . . the coffee . . . the chat . . . the cognac, of course, and the trust he had in me . . . plus the honour shown to my sister . . . all extremely . . .

"One last thing, Benjamin."

Yes, one for the road, why not?

And Marie-Colbert de Roberval, Councillor Grade One and my future brother-in-law, served me his parting shot while asking for the bill.

"Please do not take this badly, but I would rather you did not attend the wedding. Neither you, nor any member of your family."

Chapter 4

HIS ARGUMENTS STOOD up. Thérèse had told him about mum's out-of-wedlock lovers (or dumped progenitors), Clara's wedding (violent death of groom) and the union of Berthold the surgeon with our friend Mondine (brawl in the aisles of Notre Dame, seven wounded, three seriously) . . . "All of which has rather marked her, Benjamin." It wasn't that Marie-Colbert was ashamed of our family, he quite simply wanted to avoid the risk of civil war breaking out during the ceremony at Saint-Philippe-du-Roule. "Your sister just could not bear it. She has too much feeling for things sacred." (Doesn't she just.)

"But I have not plucked up the courage to mention this to Thérèse. I should prefer you to tell her, as though it were your idea. Put this small sign of cowardice down to my tact, Benjamin, I beg of you."

Julius the Dog and I chewed over all of this on the way back up to Belleville. We tried to "come to a conclusion" about our little chat, as politicians put it. But conclusions often come all on their own, thus leading to an inevitable series of consequences. The future was looking grim. And I had no need to look up to know that the copro-nimbus was following us . . .

In the end, what did all this business really come down to? Marie-Colbert de Roberval, a political animal raised on History, had decided to exploit Thérèse's gift for his own personal advancement, that's what. And this very same strategist also wanted to parachute me into the School of Schools so that later I could carry the Can of Cans. "And your job as a scapegoat, Benjamin …" Just imagine it, a National Scapegoat! What a marvellous idea for the power hungry! And didn't every politico dream of having a fortune teller to help him scrabble up the ladder, while others were blindly slipping down its rungs? No, there wasn't an ounce of sentiment in all this. It was pure calculation. Ulterior motives pushing themselves to the forefront. You do not love my sister, sir, and, to adopt your phraseology, I shall not sacrifice her on the altar of your ambition.

Our six legs wended us back up towards Belleville through a Paris in full electoral campaign, and in which Julius pissed over certain posters and not others. At first, I paid no attention. Then I couldn't believe my eyes. But there was no doubt about it, among the promising mugs with ambitious grins stuck up outside the polling stations, Julius carefully selected the ones who were to be treated to a spray of yellow urine. Half Pint and Jeremy had told me, but I thought they were only kidding.

"We trained him, Ben. Honest we did."

"He's talented. You'll see, he never misses. He's got a real political conscience."

And, by Jesus, they certainly hadn't been kidding. My two cretinous brothers had initiated Julius into the art of political sabotage! While I was busting a gut teaching them to respect other people's opinions and the wealth of diversity, they'd turned Julius into the most partisan dog in the capital!

"Stop it, Julius, for Christ's sake."

But Julius the Dog didn't stop. Julius the Dog trotted onwards and the candidates got their golden shower. Some of them, at least. Retrospective horror gripped me. What if, because of Half Pint and Jeremy, Julius had pissed all over Marie-Colbert in the Crillon? No, Julius the Dog was a French-style political animal: he only attacked images the better to get into bed with people. A two-bit conscience, in fact. A true realist. Poor pooch . . .

"Stop it, Julius!"

This time, things were getting serious. We'd reached home. For the past ten days, anonymous hands had been plastering up the angelic features of a certain Martin Lejoli on the wall opposite. Martin Lejoli promised us a monochrome France while brandishing a tricolour flame. No matter how often Jeremy, Half Pint and their gang decked him with horns or a moustache, blackened his teeth or gouged out his eyes, gave his forehead a Hitlerian fringe or transformed his flame into a monstrous phallus, the following morning Martin Lejoli arose reborn from his ashes, intact, tricoloured and smiling from a brand-new poster. Sitting on his fat arse, Julius the Dog was staring into Martin Lejoli's eyes. By the time I'd realised what he was going to do, it was too late, he was already doing it. I turned on my heels. I admit it, I denied my own dog and crept home like a coward. When I worked up the courage to lift a corner of the curtains, Martin Lejoli was steaming above a large object shaped like his flame, and Julius was scratching at the door to be let in.

All this doggy business was enough to finish me off. Thérèse would marry Marie-Colbert over my dead body. Period.

"Wanna bet?" Julie asked me.

I bet. I lost.

Thérèse knocked down my arguments one by one. The most conventional ones to begin with. This all happened over dinner. In a tribal silence. The dialogue went like this:

ME: Thérèse, do you trust me?

SHE: I trust only you, Benjamin.

ME: I just can't stomach your Marie-Colbert.

SHE: Stomaching him is my job.

ME: You know nothing about him, Thérèse.

SHE: His family has been in the history books since the seventeenth century.

ME: Politics is a risky career these days!

SHE: Can you name one career that isn't risky, these days?

ME: I mean, look at him, Thérèse! We're from different social spheres!

SHE: My social sphere is life.

ME: Handing round vol-au-vents in a Chanel tailleur is life?

SHE: No more or less than doing the washing-up in a dressing gown.

ME: He's stuck-up, Thérèse. He looks down his nose at us. He'd never been further east than the Bastille before he came to dinner here.

SHE: How often do you go to the Place de la Concorde, Benjamin?

ME: A member of his family hanged himself!

SHE: His brother would never have hanged himself if he had known you. I'm sure of that.

ME: Thérèse de Roberval ... I mean, Thérèse de Roberval, is that any name for you?

SHE: Your own son's called Monsieur Malaussène. I was against the idea, remember?

ME: Believe me, Thérèse, I've got nothing against him, but he gives me the creeps. He's as rigid as a piece of legislation!

SHE: And I'm all angles. We're made for each other.

ME: You'll be divorced in five years!

SHE: Five years of happiness? That's more than I ever expected.

Once the bourgeois method had failed, I tried to get her on her own ground.

"OK, sweetheart, let's both calm down."

"I'm perfectly calm."

"Marriage is a serious business."

"I quite agree."

"Have you taken precautions?"

"What sort of precautions?"

"Have you at least studied his horoscope? And yours? And both of yours together? Have you looked into your shared future?"

"Astrology can't do that, Benjamin."

"Can't it?"

"Astrology is for helping others, not yourself."

"Don't give me that ethical bullshit!"

"It isn't a question of ethics. The veil of love makes us blind. Even if I did try to do a tarot reading, I would be quite simply incapable. Love can't be predicted. It must be constructed. Just look at you and Julie . . ."

"Just leave Julie out of this."

(Especially since Julie was now winning her bet.) I decided to drop the diplomatic approach and hit her with the big one:

"Thérèse, Marie-Colbert has forbidden us to go to your wedding. Has he told you?"

"So what? If you're that set against the idea, he's doing you a favour, isn't he?"

No more than a second passed between my attacks and her ripostes. Finally, I decided to come clean:

"Listen, Thérèse, I took a good look at Marie-Colbert this afternoon. I didn't want to tell you this, but I left with the distinct impression that he wants to exploit your gift for his own career. He's a power-monger and this marriage is a political move!"

"You mean that he doesn't love me for myself?"

"Right. All he's interested in is the fortune teller."

"Well, that's going to be easy to check."

She pronounced that sentence so placidly that I recovered all my poise.

"I shall lose my gift the morning after my wedding night," she added. "If he casts me off, then it's because he wanted to marry a medium."

It took us some time to soak up all of the information contained in these simple words.

It was Jeremy that cracked first.

"You mean, when you're no longer a ... you won't be ..."

"Precisely."

"And so the two of you haven't ... yet, he hasn't ..."

"Bonked me? Fucked me? Screwed me? Shagged me? Laid me? Humped me?" Thérèse asked, delving into Jeremy's lexicon. "No, I've decided to be a virgin till my wedding night. Quite original in this family."

"Are you referring to mum?"

"Mum's mum. And I'm me."

And the dinner turned into a row, with Jeremy violently sticking up for mum, even though Thérèse wasn't attacking her, until the whole lot of us stormed off with a slamming of doors, just like in all the best structured families.

III

*In which it is stated that love is exactly
what it is claimed to be*

Chapter 5

I REALLY DID everything in my power to stop this wedding. First off, I chucked out Theo who was persistently standing up for Thérèse. He'd just fallen head over heels in love with a stockbroker and was claiming that passion is the only bond worth investing in. With his home-brewed logic, he came out with arguments that would have appealed to me in different circumstances:

"Let Thérèse marry her bloke, Ben. If only you knew how much Hervé and me would like to have children!"

"Do me a favour, Theo."

"Just name it."

"Go home and don't come back till I've got this sorted."

"I feel at home here, Benjamin. Hervé's been transferred to Tokyo and I can't afford to spend all day on the phone."

"We'll have a whip-round."

After that, I dealt with Jeremy, who saw me as a stubborn authority figure, opposed to a love match.

"Like the old duffers in Molière," he added.

"Jeremy, when was the last time you got a clip round the ear?"

While he was trying to remember, I made myself clear:

"Butt in again, and I'll knock the living daylight out of you.

33

OK? Oh, and while I'm at it, stop fucking about with the Martin Lejoli poster, or the musclemen that stick it back up every night will kick what's left of your brains out."

With Theo and Jeremy out of the way, I consulted my friends, one by one, like a party leader during a shake-up. Nothing doing. Even Old Sole had no idea how to stop this mess.

"You can't do anything about marriage, Benjamin. Look at my wife and me, for instance. Our families were against it. And they were right. I beat her all her life and she drank the till dry. When her cirrhosis left me a widower, I couldn't even afford a proper funeral, remember? If you hadn't been there, she'd have had a pauper's grave. And yet I miss her ... In fact it's not so much her I miss, as being married."

Julie, who'd undertaken a worldwide survey of love before meeting me, was bound to have some good advice. I asked her what she really made of Marie-Colbert. For her opinion as a woman. She replied:

"A condom."

"Sorry?"

"He's got the skin tone of a health fanatic and the fingers of a gynaecologist. He screws wearing a condom. AIDS regardless, I mean. The sort of man that never fucks with his hat off."

"I thought real politicians were sex mad, real champions of the belly truncheon."

"That doesn't necessarily make them good lovers, and it always makes them lousy husbands."

"Julie, how can I stop this?"

"Normally speaking, you can't."

"And abnormally? What if we dig up some dirt about him?"

The idea came to me as the question popped out. We'd

34

investigate Marie-Colbert de Roberval. I wanted to know every-thing about him, his career, his family, his genealogy, his reptilian brain, the works.

"If Thérèse is going to take the plunge, then she'll at least know where she's headed."

Even though Julie insisted that, in love, knowledge is a whet-stone that sharpens passions, that she'd have loved me even if she'd been shown my file, an inquisitorial gleam lit up in her eyes, and Marie-Colbert was clearly in for quite a scan.

"Don't forget his brother's death, Julie. In politics, suicides are often committed by a third party. I want to know if Charles-Henri put the noose round his own neck or whether he was strung up."

With Hadouch, Black Mo and Simon the Berber, I opened a second front. I wanted to check out the story about the Cantonese servant. Was it true that Thérèse had brought back a stray Belleville Cantonese to her husband's bed? And that this particular husband was the servant of a former minister? And that this particular minister was chums with Marie-Colbert? And was it in fact true that Marie-Colbert had consulted Thérèse in her Bohemian caravan? And if so, how many politicians had their *I Ching*s read by my sister? Since when? How far had Thérèse gone down this road? And how did these characters pay her?

Hadouch, Mo and Simon drank it all in without taking the slightest note. They were mentally sharing out the work as they listened to me. At the end of the briefing, Hadouch simply observed:

"Well, well, Ben. You're turning into a real mafioso! You're like that Corleone character in the movies."

"It's you Arabs' fault. You keep telling me I'm your brother, so now I feel like I'm one of the Family."

35

Meanwhile, I kept at Thérèse. She wasn't avoiding me, and we had several long chats about love, its mansions and its out-houses.

"You love him, you love him, but how *do you know* that you love him, Thérèse?"

"Because I can't read him. I can't see through him. All I see is him."

"The veil of love?"

"Attraction and trust, in fact."

"And what's this trust based on, for Christ's sake?"

"On attraction."

She even started going sly on me.

"You remember how you met Julie, Ben . . . When she was shoplifting pullovers?" (That's right, back when I was working at the Store with Theo.) "You who always told us not to steal . . . What exactly was your trust based on then? On her vital statistics, little brother. At the time, I too was against having her as a sister-in-law, remember?"

I remembered that very well. "With such big bosoms, how do you manage to sleep on your stomach?" Those were Thérèse's welcoming words to Julie.

"I made a mistake, Benjamin. Just as you are now making a mistake concerning Marie-Colbert."

(Marie-Colbert . . . I was never going to get used to that.)

After-dinner chats. With Thérèse and I going down Boulevard de Belleville, passing by the Zebra, up for sale for so long but still unbought, as though it was sacred, but doomed to be flogged off in the end, because nothing is really sacred, not even that shell of a cinema, or that tall bag of bones walking beside me, who was being hailed by the passers-by as a familiar figure, and who an aristocratic bastard was now inching towards playing some sinister role . . .

"Watch out, Benjamin, I know what you're thinking."

She giggled.

"Don't forget, I'm still a virgin."

Then we set off back via Rue de l'Orillon, where Jeremy, Half Pint and their mates were playing basketball in a fenced-off yard, a foretaste of our coming Bronx. On other occasions, we went up Rue Ramponneau, where the new Belleville, dead on delivery with its autistic architecture lay opposite the old Belleville, swarming with noisy existence, Jewish mothers hailing Thérèse, their sumptuous arses spilling over the edges of their chairs, thanking her for having sorted out "you know what", inviting us to share their tea or offering us pine seeds and mint so we could make some at home: "Come on young lady, on my mother's life, it's a gift from the heart!", or we stamped up Rue de Belleville as far as Métro Pyrénées, a long march through China, with more eternal gratitude for Thérèse, shrimp fritters, bottles of Nuok-Mam, "*Yao buyao fan*, Thérèse? (You want some rice, Thérèse?) Yes, yes! Take, take! It's a pweasure for me!", then Turkish biscuits from the Turks, with a bottle of raki thrown in, we had a large shopping bag with us, Thérèse refused nothing, it was her way of having the locals pay her, an old-time priest feeding on the poultry offered for absolution . . .

"I'm going to invite them all," she announced one evening.

"Invite them?"

"To my wedding. All of my customers. Marie-Colbert will like that."

"You reckon?"

"I'm sure of it."

All of Belleville invading Saint-Philippe-du-Roule instead of the undesirable Malaussène clan seemed like a great idea to me, but I wasn't so sure about Marie-Colbert . . .

"You're wrong about that, Benjamin. I know a few things about Marie-Colbert that you do not . . ."

For instance, that he was sufficiently broad-minded to recruit the bridesmaids from among Gervaise's whorelets.

"What?"

"That's right, Benjamin. He went with me to Passion Fruit and personally asked Gervaise to choose our bridesmaids and pageboys. He feels very concerned about deprived children. Just ask Clara."

That said while bagging the evening papers which our friend Azzouz gave us on Rue des Pyrénées before shutting up his shop.

Concerning the customers who were to be invited to the wedding, Thérèse resumed:

"I owe it to them. Because I'll be of no further use to them after my wedding night."

True. I'd forgotten about that. Loss of gift upon loss of cherry. Did Thérèse actually believe such bullshit? It really bugged me. I looked in vain for the reason why the upbringing I'd given her had launched her so far up into the stars, how old she'd been when it had all started, and why . . . But her pat answers took the wind out of my sails.

"How did it all start? With my periods of course!"

When I rather snidely pointed out that her fortune-telling gifts had never saved us from the slightest catastrophe, she hit back with her inevitable veil of love: "Love makes us blind, Benjamin, love *must* make us blind! It has its own dazzling light."

In other words, divination for the family, friends and oneself was a case of insider trading.

"Something like that, yes."

That's when I decided to pull a fast one on her. During that very conversation. I'm not particularly proud of the fact, but I had no choice. My thinking was simple. If Thérèse couldn't predict her own future, or that of MC2, I'd send her along someone else, a woman, a complete stranger, with exactly the same astral references as her: same time, date and place of birth, plus those of de Roberval. The stranger would pass all this off as genuine data concerning her own marriage, and Thérèse would foresee her own future while thinking it was for another couple. Since she believed all that crap, she'd then have the evidence in front of her eyes.

"You realise you're a complete bastard?" Hadouch asked me.

"Just find me the girl for the job and leave me to deal with my conscience."

(So I really was turning into a mini mafioso. A two-bit shitty godfather.)

"That's easy. Rachida, Kader the cabby's daughter. She's just been dumped by a copper who screwed her round something rotten. A burglar cop, believe it or not. Even though she's a research assistant, she didn't look into her lover-boy enough. She should have gone for a tarot reading before getting wed. She'll do that for Thérèse."

Chapter 6

I T WAS JULIE who reported back first.

"Where do you want me to start, Benjamin? With today's Marie-Colbert, or his ancestors? Shall we take the current of history upstream, or downstream?"

"Chronologically, Julie. The good old family tree from the top right down to this very minute."

And so Julie presented her findings, which I reproduce here in all their historical dryness:

"To begin, Marie-Colbert is an inherited first name, passed down from one generation to the next. As you'll see, we're up to our eyeballs in politics right from the start. The first Marie-Colbert was born during the reign of Louis XIV, in about 1660, the fruit of a liaison between a certain Comte de Roberval and Colbert's niece. This de Roberval made a great contribution to Colbert's victory over Fouquet. He so thoroughly rigged the Superintendent's show trial that Fouquet was carted straight off to the State Prison of Pignerol where, as you know, he died in mysterious circumstances."

"Another assisted suicide?"

"Definitely. As a result, the Comte de Roberval inherited some of Fouquet's property, and called his son Marie-Colbert as a tribute to his lord and master. End of Act I, or *the origins of a fortune founded on silence.* Act II, fifty years or so later, little Marie-Colbert had now become the director of the *Compagnie d'Occident,* the main player behind Law's bankruptcy. But he had been wise enough to marry one of the Pâris girls (the Pâris family were responsible for Law's downfall, after he had been denounced by Marie-Colbert) and, as a reward, he picked up the entire Rue de Quincampoix – where Marie-Colbert still lives, in their town house at number 60. In Act III, you have a Marie-Colbert under each regime. Talleyrand alone employed three of them (they died young but reproduced rapidly): one to vote through the confiscation of church property and pocket a chunk of it in the name of the nation; the second to manage the booty Napoleon had picked up during his European campaigns (he was in charge of a secret ministry for this very reason); and the third in 1830 to betray the Restoration in favour of the Orleanist party once the price was right. End of Act III. The family fortune is now incalculable. Act IV, 1887, the Third Republic and the Panama Canal; having been bribed by Reinach the banker, another Marie-Colbert busied himself in parliament getting support for a loan which would ruin 800,000 subscribers and make him even richer. The inquiry whitewashed Marie-Colbert, but led to the condemnation of Baïhaut the minister, after he'd been denounced, and the death of Reinach the banker."

"Suicide?"

"History says that he was found dead at his home. But wait for the other two scenes in this act. Firstly, the presence of a Marie-Colbert during the Stavisky scandal at the end of 1933, then ten years later the very same Marie-Colbert served on the Jewish

Affairs Commission for the confiscation of property! This was our Marie-Colbert's grandfather. Note that in the Stavisky affair (several tens of millions of francs' worth of saving certificates issued by the Crédit Municipal of Bayonne and backed up by stolen jewels) the Marie-Colbert in question was also the son-in-law of Hamelster the jeweller, who was robbed down to his last emerald and then hanged himself."

"A lot of hangings and a lot of denunciations . . ."

"Don't call the Comtes de Roberval grasses, my love. I shan't let you utter such an unpleasant word."

"They're a dynasty of crooks, that much is for sure."

"Or with a long family tradition in finance, it depends how you look at it."

"What about our one? I mean, Thérèse's one?"

"That's where I'm going to disappoint you, Benjamin."

What she then told me should have delighted me. But, lord alone knows why, I felt distinctly let down.

"Our Marie-Colbert is the enormous exception that breaks the rule. What do I mean 'breaks'? He abolishes it! Totally wipes it out! Our Marie-Colbert is a saint. From the First-Aid Certificate he got when he was twelve, to his humanitarian work on the world's battlefields, amid embargoes and in natural disaster areas, he has shown himself to be all the more irreproachable since, unlike other benefactors, he has always been extremely discreet and utterly efficient."

"But what about the hanged brother?"

"He was depressed. I found the doctor who was treating him. His wife had just left him. He was in love, Benjamin, like you."

"So Marie-Colbert is a true saint."

"Compassion made flesh."

42

*

Hadouch had come to a similar conclusion.

"You're barking up the wrong tree here, Ben. Simon found the Cantonese couple, and Thérèse definitely did make them drink her love potion. The servant's master, the minister, didn't consult your sister personally, but he did send along Marie-Colbert, who was going crazy after his brother's death. That was over a year back and, as far as I know, no other politician from the old, present or future government has seen Thérèse since. As regards wages, Thérèse agreed to be paid as usual with food, offcuts of cloth, trinkets, but generally she refuses, saying that she isn't there to earn money, but to help those in need. She reckons that it's her generosity that 'regenerates her gift' (don't look at me like that, Ben, those were her very words) and that mediums who ask for payment are obviously charlatans because greed makes us all blind. However, her abilities are apparently universal, and if you don't mind me saying so, she could be raking it in if she wanted. She uses every sort of divination, from direct clairvoyance to oenomancy, including rhabdomancy, the tarot, a crystal ball, chiromancy, the laying on of hands, the *I Ching*, coffee grounds, sand readings, sea-shells, runes, and so on and so forth. There's something for every ethnic group in Belleville . . . But that's not all . . . Hang on to your hat . . ."

We were sitting in Amar's. Beside us, Old Sole was gobbling up his daily merguez couscous.

"Why do you refuse to believe in things like that, Benjamin?" he asked me while Hadouch was getting his breath back. "I consult Thérèse every week! And she never fails me!"

An evil thought crossed my mind concerning Sole, his merguez couscous, his tattered suit and battered shoes . . . I was wondering

43

what he'd look like if Thérèse ever did fail him. And, in a more general way, I was wondering where this god-awful century was headed, and if Thérèse was out to blow up the last ramparts of a universe that was tottering on the brink of the irrational. Sole gave me one of his leftover smiles:

"She wants me to be a witness at her wedding, did you know that?"

I was about to congratulate him, when he added beaming radiantly:

"That means I'm going to be on telly!"

"On telly?"

"Hasn't Thérèse told you? They're going to film the wedding. It's going to be broadcast the next day. That way, me, her customers and all the other guests will be on telly!"

"What?"

Sole's face drew near, an archangelic gleam in his eyes.

"It's to help the poor, Benjamin. And Gervaise's whores' kids up there at Passion Fruit."

To judge by Hadouch's laughter, my face must have been quite a sight.

"Ah yes, my brother, the grand charity wedding. The kind of thing that draws the cameras in times of high unemployment. The Malaussène tribe has not been invited, but we'll be able to watch Thérèse's wedding as a nice bit of family viewing on Sunday evening."

I felt myself drain to grey. Hadouch laid his hand on my arm.

"Don't faint yet. You still haven't heard the best bit . . ."

". . ."

"The best bit of all, my brother, is that since Thérèse met Marie-Colbert, her little caravan has become a humanitarian centre."

And Hadouch explained how, apart from her predictions, Thérèse gave the mysterious messengers sent to her by Marie-Colbert stocks of drugs, ready-to-use infirmaries, batches of schoolbooks and so on, in other words she and Marie-Colbert were treating, clothing, feeding and teaching entire populations which tin-pot tyrants and well-meant embargoes had left to die in various parts of the world. This was done secretly, so as not to offend the governments in question, but it was a large-scale operation. It was the Marie-Colbert method.

"..."

"..."

There we were, then. Shame on me! Sorry, Marie-Colbert. And Thérèse, oh my Thérèse, please forgive me. Alleluia, go in peace, may God bless you and I'll eat my hat. It pisses me off to say so, but I'm no longer against your wedding.

When Rachida Kader, the research assistant, met up with me at the Deux Rives, Areski's couscous eatery on Rue des Pyrénées, I'd given up the fight. The expression on her face and her opening words confirmed my defeat.

"So, I went to see your sister, but I must tell you straightaway that you're not going to like what I found out, Monsieur Malaussène."

I raised a fatalistic hand.

"Call me Benjamin. It'll help the medicine go down."

Areski had placed us at the back of his restaurant on the round table. Our little chat was completely confidential.

"OK, Benjamin. But just so as there'll be no misunderstanding, I don't believe a word of this astrology bullshit."

She was a fiery, wonderful girl. Before getting to the crux

45

of the matter, she was stating her position.

"I admire Thérèse for all the good she does, but I'm a shop steward in a company where we're fighting against recruitment using numerology, horoscopes, graphology, psychomorphology and so on . . ."

Rachida looked like one of the portraits of Berber women that Areski had hung on the walls of his restaurant – straight and uncolonisable. Right from the start, she got lucidly stroppy:

"Even when I was a little girl I hated Saint-Exupéry's *The Little Prince*. And today I can confirm that his fable is a lie. Bankers don't count stars! And when they consult them, it's so they can take on their wife's runt of a nephew instead of someone qualified. Do you know what, Malaussène? Divination in all its forms is an excuse for nepotism in companies. We should behead the head-hunters and advise job applicants to invent for themselves the horoscope of an eternal whiz-kid. That's what your sister Thérèse ought to be doing! We should blow this crap to pieces from within."

To be perfectly honest with you, Julie, I took a fancy to Rachida. I just adored her magnificent ardour. Another Julie, to a 'T'. A wonderful shit-stirrer. Just like you used to be. When Areski came to take our order, we went for two makfouls and a bottle of rosé. I then asked:

"So, tell me Rachida, given your opinion of astrology, why did you agree to do me this favour?"

"For two reasons. Firstly because Hadouch asked me, and Hadouch is very important to me. And secondly because Thérèse believes in it, so I thought if I can help her to avoid the sort of marriage I've just been through, then anything is worth a go."

46

"And the result?"

She looked at me, opened her mouth, changed her mind, then handed me an envelope.

"That's for you to decide. Thérèse wrote it all down."

IV

In which we see that even the stars are deceitful in love

Chapter 7

W E DON'T WANT what we really want. There's an end to it.
I should have jumped with joy when reading the astral
decree Thérèse had given Rachida. But I didn't. I was wallowing
in sadness from the first line:

"*A marriage with Jupiter in transit in the 7th House indicates a
deceitful and destructive husband,*" wrote Thérèse in that seismo-
graphic hand she used when taking dictation from the stars.
"*The Pluto-Uranus conjunction indicates early widowhood . . .*" Jesus
Christ, "early widowhood" in black and white before my very
eyes . . . Marie-Colbert's death, just like with Clara's Clarence . . .

And so on down the entire page on which Thérèse had unwit-
tingly described the disasters heaven had in store for her. Then,
of course, to cap it all: "*However a harmonious aspect in the 5th
House indicates the likelihood of a birth . . .*" Likelihood? Knowing
the Malaussène tribe, 'likely births' are dead certainties, we could
already start buying in nappies and sterilising bottles. But what a
lovely style the stars had! What marvellous heavenly bureaucracy!
"*Mercury in the 9th House gives promise of a short trip abroad . . .
Comparison with the 2nd House suggests a country with a large
banking sector.*" And what preoccupations! 'A large banking sector'!

Sex, money and more sex . . . O purity of the heavenly vault!

So, I should have jumped with joy as I read that. Thérèse had been saved. This astral judgment was enough to open even the most thoroughly love-blinkered eyes. We'd save on the trousseau and the stamp duty for the divorce papers. Thérèse, you're surely not going to wed a bloke in whom *"Jupiter is in dissonance with Pluto"*! Are you, now? Especially considering that the very same geezer has somehow managed to lodge *"Mars and Uranus in the 8th House"*, which guarantees him a *"sudden violent death"*! Come on now, Thérèse, do be reasonable!

But I didn't really find it all that funny. The fact that I didn't believe in all this starry claptrap didn't detract from the fact that Thérèse certainly did. With empathy firing on all cylinders, the brother then drowned in his sister's future tears. Not to mention the feeling of betrayal. This indiscretion which Thérèse would never forgive me for . . . A cosmic rape . . . Astral incest . . . Oh Thérèse, forgive me for the good I'm going to do you!

As this was a professional matter, I didn't want to raise it with Thérèse at home. With the fatal envelope in my breast pocket, I went to wait my turn in the queue outside her Bohemian caravan. Of course, it then started to rain. Curious about its future, Belleville society was floundering in the mud. To our left, Père-Lachaise knew where we were all going to end up, and on the other side of the Boulevard Letrou Undertakers (yes Letrou, 'the hole', go and see for yourselves if you don't believe me) was already displaying our marble slabs. You can't blame funeral parlours for opening up in front of cemeteries. It's the obscenity of allegory. Babywear stores below maternity clinics, Job Centres beside schools, Martin Lejoli's headquarters next to the Job Centre, the barracks a little further on, and Letrou Undertakers opposite Père-Lachaise cemetery . . . It's the order of things.

What if I forgot the whole thing? Even if I did manage to stop Thérèse's marriage, would it prevent the rest from coming true? The whole lot? That fateful chain of events?

"What's up, Benjamin?"

I jumped.

"What's up? You consult Thérèse as well now, do you?"

Old Sole had just laid his hand on my sleeve.

"Do you know what she's just told me?"

He'd just emerged from the caravan.

"She told me that, after her wedding night, she won't be able to see the future any more."

He was staring at a puddle at his feet.

"That's bad news for me."

His shoes were too old to be playing with that puddle. With his sodden head, he nodded at that long queue.

"And it must be bad news for everybody here . . ."

'Everybody here' was dripping into the mud.

I smothered a sneer, but couldn't help remarking:

"You'll all going to be on telly, Sole, that's quite some consolation."

It was an ecumenical caravan. Crucifixes of every shape, variously coloured Fatima's hands, with florescent constellations stuck to the ceiling and a zodiac menagerie embroidered on the curtains. There was something for every breed of despair.

"Thérèse, I've done something that I . . ."

A whispered confession in the penumbra between two worlds, reddened by a candle flame below the statue of Yemanja. This candle never went out. At the darkest hour of the night, Yemanja watched over Belleville.

53

"Thérèse, I've done something you're going to hate me for."

I placed the envelope in front of her. Without pausing for breath, I explained the set-up. I repeated over and over that it had nothing to do with Rachida, that the whole thing had been worked out by me for Thérèse's own good, because she hadn't trusted my fraternal instinct, and as a result I'd fallen back on the stars so she could judge for herself objectively ... sorry ... but there we are ...

The Thérèse listening to me from the other side of a purple table wasn't done up like a medium. No jewellery, no veil, no turban, nothing fancy. It was just plain Thérèse. Our Thérèse with her cheeks a bit more hollowed out by the half-light, maybe, but with the same angles and the same electric voice.

"No, Benjamin, I don't hold this against you. On the other hand, I'm not going to thank you for it either. You just did your brotherly duty."

The same bureaucratic eloquence. She glanced at the envelope lying on the cashmere tablecloth. She didn't touch it. She just changed the subject:

"Do you remember who gave me this Yemanja?"

She'd turned round to face the statuette. No, I couldn't remember.

"A Brazilian transvestite."

Bingo! It was a Brazilian drag queen, one of Theo's little play-mates. From the good old days of the whores from the Bois de Boulogne.

"Exactly. And do you remember what that transvestite said when he saw me for the first time?"

"No, you've got me there."

"He said, in Portuguese: *Essa mossa chorava na barriga da mãe.*

54

He said that I cried while still in my mother's womb. This was the first sign that I was clairvoyant, Benjamin."

Then, coming back to the subject of our conversation:

"Did Rachida explain to you how I drew up this double horoscope?"

"With the information I'd given her, I suppose."

"I'm talking about the *technique*, Benjamin. Did she tell you which *technique* I used? *How* I proceeded?"

No, Rachida had been interested only in the result.

"It was a laying-on of hands. I didn't open the envelope. I left it on the table, just where it is now, and placed my hands on it. An envelope laid there by a woman in pain. The paper was impregnated with Rachida's suffering. Even if the envelope had been empty, my conclusions would have been the same. Rachida was pure torment. Anger and torment. It was not the future of my marriage that I saw when I touched that envelope soaked in suffering. It was the past of her marriage."

(What? Come again? Pardon? I didn't quite catch that . . .)

But Thérèse did not repeat what she'd said, she pressed further on. Rachida's copper had indeed been a "destructive" and extremely "deceitful" hubby! With bags of charm, of course, and youthful good looks which fooled most people, but he had a "brutal and unscrupulous character", which had been more than she could take and which would doubtlessly put him at the wrong end of a charge sheet one of these days.

"But . . . the trip abroad . . ." I said. "The country with a large banking sector . . ."

"That's the funniest part of the story, Benjamin. Eric – her policeman was called Eric, by the way – took Rachida to Monaco. He's an obsessive gambler. One night, after losing a fortune, he decided to burgle the flat of an old lady gambler who was away for the weekend. The flat had a special security system. Its automatic doors and steel blinds trapped Eric until the Monegasque police force showed up."

I pathetically played my last card.

"What about the predicted pregnancy?"

"Rachida's already pregnant. She'll either abort, or else Hadouch will adopt it. I'd put my money on the latter possibility."

"Hadouch and Rachida?"

"Yes, I think things will turn out better with the bad guy than with the constable. A moral you ought to approve of, little brother."

Thérèse looked at the envelope on the table and grinned.

"So Rachida's envelope contained my birth-date and that of Marie-Colbert? That's something I'd never have foreseen!"

Chapter 8

THE FOLLOWING EVENING, the copro-nimbus which had been dogging me since that chat at the Crillon dumped its load on me. I woke up screaming. Julie switched the light on at once. But nothing could be more brightly illumined than my mind.

"I know what's going to happen, Julie."

And then I told her:

"Thérèse is going to marry our Marie-Colbert de Roberval, a real-life saint, just like Clara's Clarence was, and Marie-Colbert is going to get gunned down, just like Clara's Clarence was. Then I'm going to be accused of murder and get banged up. This time, I'm really going to cop it. I'm going to have the entire political world on my arse and Coudrier isn't going to unretire himself again to get me off. Nine months later, the Malaussène tribe will inherit another lodger who will emerge from Thérèse's loins while I'm in the slammer. That's what's going to happen."

"Business as usual, then."

That's all Julie came out with before turning the light off and going back to sleep.

But I didn't go back to sleep. I got up and started to think things over in front of the window. 'Business as usual' ... There was something horribly true in her piss-take. It wasn't just the fact that our tribal history had been preordained by the cumbersome hand of fate, it was more that History in general, the one with the capital H, definitely did repeat itself whatever you say, think, compute, analyse, conclude, forecast, decide, vote, do or commemorate. History then repeats itself from bad to worse, as can be seen in the bastardly angelic looks of Martin Lejoli pasted up on the wall over the road through the slanting rain, in the orange of the street lamps and the certainty of his final victory. And so, and so . . . my heart beats stammered . . . thanks to this constant repetition, humanity is finally going to scupper itself in the not too far distant future. And me with it.

Yes, the time would soon come when I'd be ending my days in the slammer.

And something told me that the time was now ripe.

So why not get used to the idea right away?

The next day, during breakfast, no-one dared ask me what I was thinking about. I barely moistened my lips with my coffee before leaving the hardware shop without uttering a word. I went to the Vendetta Press, where I shared the lift with Queen Zabo.

"I thought I'd fired you, Malaussène."

"Correct, your Majesty. And you were right to do so. I'm just here for a consultation."

"In that case . . ."

She showed me into her office. I asked for coffee and the presence of my friend Loussa de Casamance.

"If I understand you correctly," Queen Zabo summed up when I'd finished speaking, "you are going to be sent down for a long stretch for the murder of an ephemeral brother-in-law, a

Councillor with the Audit Office, is that it?"

"A Grade One one, that's right."

"And, as usual, we'd be wasting our time if we tried to convince you that you're talking complete crap?" Loussa asked.

"So tell us what we can do for you, my lad."

"Give me an inexhaustible library, your Majesty. Books that will take me through a life sentence."

That was my idea. I wanted the two of them to come up with the jail-bird's perfect library. And I must say they got quite carried away. To begin with, Loussa reeled off some escapist titles, in the true sense of the word, and suggested that I re-read *The Count of Monte-Cristo* and *Papillon*. But then Queen Zabo pointed out that I wasn't the sort who'd dig tunnels with his fingernails and that such a whiff of fresh air would only do my head in.

"No, Malaussène, when one is cramped at home, one shouldn't try to expand. One should see the bright side of its limitations."

Her rather convincing idea was that someone locked up for the rest of his life, in a cell measuring three yards by two, should only read books about confinement.

"The great mystics, for instance. John of the Cross. Ever heard of John of the Cross, Malaussène? Does *The Dark Night of the Soul* mean anything to you?"

"Or else, in a different register," Loussa butted in, "how about Erving Goffman? Have you ever read Goffman's *Asylums*? It's an essay about asylums and other confined spaces. Just the ticket for you, shit-for-brains. It will give you the key to unlock everybody else's behaviour in the penitential universe. And if they ever let you out, you would then have no problem getting yourself sectioned in a bin or volunteering to serve in a nuclear submarine. *Ba mian ling long*, as the Chinese say. Adapt to your surroundings."

I must say my morning wasn't wasted. Queen Zabo and Loussa de Casamance piled all the available concentration-camp literature on me, from Robert Antelme and Primo Levi to Chalamov's *Tales of the Kolima*, including everything that the Chinese had done to other Chinese, and in more general terms mankind to itself in this century of big ideas.

"And then you can re-read Sartre's *The Wall*," Loussa advised me.

"And Huysmans's *A rebours*," Queen Zabo added, then they ping-ponged away merrily: *The Castle, The Magic Mountain, Robinson Crusoe, The Diary of a Madman,* Jouve's *Paulina* with her double incarnation, *The Royal Game, The Conscience of Zeno, Watching and Punishing,* a good hundred titles that I immediately ordered from Azzouz my newsagent, while warning him not to make any snide comments.

"Oh, and you should add Cioran's notebooks," Loussa concluded. "You know Cioran, don't you? A Romanian who carried his own prison round with him. You'll see. He makes some interesting points about the futility of escaping."

Queen Zabo disagreed:

"Not at all. He had the key to his cell in his pocket, but didn't dare use it, which is totally different!"

The following weeks sped by with the two-fold preparations of Thérèse's wedding and my incarceration. As regards Thérèse, everyone chipped in with their advice:

"There's just one thing you need to remember so that you won't look a complete twot in high society," Jeremy said. "Knife to the right, and fork to the left."

"With the fork's prongs facing downwards," Louna pointed out. "It's the English who lay their forks upside down."

Friend Theo was all of a tizzy:

"As for your bridal gown, put yourself in my capable hands. Come here so I can measure you, darling."

"Theo, you really are a *dear*," Thérèse exclaimed in the fake lovey-dovey tone of her new circle.

"I'll start rehearsing the bridesmaids and pageboys tomorrow," Gervaise promised.

As for me, I'd traded in Julie's bed for an inflatable mattress on the kids' floor. Since I was going to be remanded for years of over-populated custody, I'd may as well get used to sleeping through Half Pint's groans, Jeremy's curses, Thérèse galvanic spasms, Verdun's untimely awakenings and Julius the Dog's stench. Clara, What An Angel and Monsieur Malaussène were problem-free and slumbered like logs – even in the worst cells there must be two or three loonies that slept normally.

While the family was benefiting from the cookery classes Clara was giving Thérèse – Thérèse had been told that a husband marches on his stomach – I was eating bottled eggs laid on a sump of spinach.

"What are you doing?" asked Half Pint, who was about to puke.

"I'm on a diet."

"Are you ill?" Jeremy asked.

"I'm inoculating myself."

"You're what?"

Whatever the context, I'd adopted the laconic aggressiveness of the tattooed jailbirds Jeremy and Half Pint loved to see in their Sunday matinée American movies. They were pleased I'd decided to go along with them.

"So you've finally got interested in the pictures, Ben?"

61

"Fuck you."

Nobody really understood what I was up to. I was on a secret training scheme. True heroism consists in anticipating the worst while not sharing the pain caused by that anticipation. Anyway, if I had to tell them that I was going to get locked up, they probably wouldn't have given a toss. Everyone had a bee in his or her bonnet. Thérèse with her wedding, everyone else with Thérèse's wedding and Julie with the blockbuster she was going to write about Marie-Colbert's delightful family.

"I've unearthed another one, this time in 1954, Benjamin, at the end of the war in Indochina. The groom's father. He was up to his neck in the piastre scandal."

Meanwhile, Thérèse was getting prouder and prouder of her very own Marie-Colbert:

"Marie-Colbert's had a marvellous idea! Instead of asking for expensive wedding presents, we're going to ask for cheap ones!"

(Marvellous idea, that . . .)

"And as our guests are pretty hard up, he's bought them all himself! They'll all just have to pick out the present they want to give, but without spending a centime. Isn't that marvellous?"

That night, I felt like getting myself chained up in the cellar.

Then Julie cracked. When I asked her to embroider my initials on my prison pyjamas, she cracked.

"Not that, Malaussène! Don't tell me you're *really* in training for your sentence! [She only calls me Malaussène and speaks in italics when pushed to the limit.] I thought you were just pretending! So this isn't a game? You're serious, are you? You really are as big a dickhead as you look? In that case, just piss off! Go and train somewhere else! Go and whack de Roberval while

62

you're at it! That way, you'll be judged for something you've really done for once in your life!"

She was absolutely fuming. I realised she was about to kick arse.

"What the fuck am I doing with Mr Humanitarian Preacherman? Am I soft in the head, or what? This compassion freak, this empathy dictator, a masochist who bleeds himself dry, only fit for wearing a crown of thorns and looking like the Turin Shroud whenever life doesn't come up to his nicety nice ideals!"

She opened a suitcase.

"You're going to the slammer, Malaussène? Want me to pack for you?"

She started chucking in whatever came to hand – including a full ashtray.

"We'll call a cab to take you to Sing Sing while we're waiting for your brother-in-law to buy it. That way, you can practise getting anally raped! Because that's what prison really means, wise guy! It's not only about smelly feet, spinach and bottled eggs!"

I must have looked a bit off.

Because she stopped.

She thought it over.

Then she unbuckled my belt.

She'd shrilled out and was now purring.

"If I was you, Benjamin, if I was really worried about copping a life sentence, my preparation would be rather different. I'd go for tits and arse, I'd fuck till my balls ached, I'd go for the best restaurants, best films, best plays, best laughs, I'd give myself such a high that I'd need more than a life sentence to bring me down again . . ."

I thought about all that while she was tossing our clothes away.

I decided to adopt her strategy.

At least until Thérèse's wedding.

V

Of the wedding
Of what happened before and of what of course
happened after

Chapter 9

THE LAST TIME I saw Thérèse as a maiden was when she was plunging into the bridal gown Theo was holding out. 'Plunge' is the right word. It was a dark blue dress which swallowed my astral sister up as if she'd leapt down from the heavens into a bottomless sea. Then her head and hands miraculously re-emerged and the dress lit up! Gervaise's charges and our little ones, who were sitting in a semicircle as though surrounding a birthday party magician, went "Ooh!" and "Ah!"

"The Great Bear!"

"Andromeda!"

"The Orion nebula!"

All this was Theo's bright idea. He'd decked that nocturnal fabric with all the constellations which cluttered up Thérèse's head. The whorelet bridesmaids, who'd been taught all about the night sky, had a great time identifying them while the bride twirled round like a spaceship in zero gravity.

"Cassiopeia!"

"Eridanus!"

"Sculptor!"

"Piscis Australis!"

"Taurus! Taurus!"

A flashing heavenly vault, topped by the bride's radiant face, on which Theo placed an aureole of pale fire, which Half Pint recognised at once:

"It's the Corona Borealis! It's the Corona Borealis! I said it first!"

He'd been faster than the passion fruit on this one, and wanted us all to know. Theo awarded him his astronomer's diploma:

"You're right, Half Pint."

Then, turning to me:

"So, Ben, what do you reckon?"

It was high time Theo got himself a job sprinkling fairy dust for Walt Disney, that's what I reckoned.

"Don't be such a hypocrite, Ben, you love the dress and you just won't admit it! This dress is absolutely lustrous, my dear . . . By the way", he whispered into my ear, "do you know what it's going to earn me?"

". . . ?"

"Two days in Hervé's arms, that's what. Marie-Colbert insisted on inviting him over for a weekend in bed. Tokyo–Paris in business class. It's just as well, the poor lad was at bursting point. Me, too, for that matter."

Well, Marie-Colbert certainly did seem to possess every conceivable good quality.

"Wait, you haven't seen the best bit yet!"

The best bit was the bride's train, which was supposed to depict Halley's comet. This luminous tail was soon to be rolled out in the forecourt of Saint-Philippe-du-Roule in full view of the cameras. The whorelet bridesmaids, who Theo had dressed up as shooting stars, were holding it up with the tips of the gilded fingers.

The time has now come to talk about that TV show, that conjugal-cum-charitable high mass, the fucking icing on this grotesque wedding cake. When I pointed out to Thérèse that there was a distinct lack of intimacy in all this carry-on, she replied that by marrying Marie-Colbert, she was espousing a cause, and that all good causes needed publicity.

"Marriage is always a commitment, Benjamin, and any commitment is a denial of the self. It's just a bit more of a denial for me, that's all. Let's just say I'm sacrificing myself live."

Joan of Arc gets wed, in fact.

As a result, on Sunday evening, the day after the happy event, I witnessed the showing of my sister's wedding along with several million other viewers. Filmed as *a live outside broadcast*, if you don't mind. Apparently, it was so 'live' that the director had asked the wedding party to enter then leave the church ten times over, as though in the grip of some strange spell.

It was a mild evening. Amar, Hadouch, Mo and Simon had perched the Koutoubia's telly in a tree on the boulevard then put chairs and tables all round it on the pavement. All of Belleville showed up. The guests and the rest. A syncretic odour of lacquered duck and roast mutton united the crowd in a mutual fragrance of coriander. Rabbi Razon provided Kosher Bordeaux for the entire assembly – his contribution to Thérèse's nuptials. Everyone was eating, drinking and going wild, with their eyes glued to the screen.

"Thérèse predicted that I'd be on telly one day!"

"Me too!"

Not only had Thérèse invited them to her wedding, she had raised them to the glory of the gogglebox! Around that tree, there was an atmosphere of eternal gratitude.

69

"There's no getting away from it," Hadouch said ironically, "your brother-in-law sure knows how to throw a party."

What my brother-in-law knew how to do more than anything else was pull an impressive number of strings. From what the syrupy commentator said, it was clear that this film had been commissioned long ago, carefully prepared then shot so that the slightest detail was in praise of Marie-Colbert de Roberval, and him alone, "*such a discreet patron of charities, so taken up by his activities on every field of human suffering*" (sic), that he now stood for "*the lost honour of a political class that has long been discredited by scandals*" (sic again). Yes, this "*unknown man risen from nowhere* (hadn't he just!) *who, during the previous government, refused a ministerial post and instead joined the austerity of the Audit Office, in order to devote his free time to the sufferings of the world*" (what a guy!), embodied a political renewal "*for which the French nation had given up all hope*".

All this in a long tremolo, while the eye of the camera glided over the "*humble and multi-ethnic folk*" ("humble and multi-ethnic folk", his very words!) who were awaiting the arrival of the "*nuptial couple*".

Old Sole gently elbowed me.

"Look, Benjamin, this is where it gets really beautiful!"

The "really beautiful" appeared on the box in the shape of an ambulance. Thérèse and Marie-Colbert were getting married in an ambulance!

"A GMC," Old Sole pointed out. "The 33 model, revised in '42, and specially equipped for the Red Cross. As solid as they come."

An historically symbolic ambulance, then, with a vertical windscreen, large notched tyres and half-moon windows at the back, as seen in newsreels of Paris liberating itself.

"Marie-Colbert has more imagination than you credit him with," Thérèse had warned me.

I now saw her emerge from the ambulance, while Marie-Colbert in a white tuxedo and top-hat held out a gloved hand.

Around me, the crowd joined their cheers with those that had been produced the day before during this live outside broadcast.

"Come on, Julius, let's go home."

I didn't want to see the rest. The more telly envisions a surprise, the less surprising it is. This is because of its paunch-like nature. Paunches don't surprise, they digest. Sometimes they puke, which is about as surprising as they can get. I could have trotted out the remainder of that voice-over without even looking at the pictures: a few more gushes about Marie-Colbert's love for humanity, a certificate of authenticity issued by a couple of VIPs, who were moved to tears, the solemn entry into the church (Bach, natürlich), the cohort of "humble and multi-ethnic folk", their eyes suddenly dilated by such divine splendour, a sermon delivered by the priest – in this case a bishop, probably the groom's cousin – concerning the right hand of God, reserved for the long-term unemployed for all eternity, doling out of communion, a timid "I do" from the bride and a firm "I do" from the groom, *Deo gratias*, then departure in the white ambulance (more Bach) for a honeymoon in a destination *"which we shall keep secret out of respect for their privacy"*. Except that I knew where it was. That plonker of a Marie-Colbert was taking Thérèse to Zurich.

(Zurich!)

"All the same, it's more original than Venice," Jeremy exclaimed after I'd gone into a sulk.

And now that Julius and I were alone in our hardware shop,

now that I was sitting on Thérèse's bed, plunged up to my eyeballs in gloom, the very thought of Zurich wrung my heart. I thought of a book I'd read long ago, but never really got over, which Loussa and Queen Zabo had forgotten to put on my prison reading list. Its title was *Mars*, and it told in grizzly detail how a young man called Fritz Zorn dies of a terrible cancer which he thinks he contracted from an over-long adolescence spent on the gilded shores of the lake in Zurich. Fritz Zorn claimed that love was mankind's honour, that the splendid individuals living by that lake had deprived him of this honour, and that was what was killing him.

And it was to the scene of his death throes that Marie-Colbert was going to teach my sister how to love!

That night, untangling the threads of our recent conversations, I fell asleep on Thérèse's bed.

"I know why you don't like Marie-Colbert, Benjamin: he isn't sentimental, but he's a good man. Though he looks like a budding senator, he isn't even a real adult yet. To get what he wants, he needs to have the faith of a young man. You suspect him of thinking only of himself, when in fact he's doing all he can to make up for the damage done by a family that has always lived for itself. You criticise his political ambitions ... but aren't you a political animal yourself, little brother? You says he's got a 'classy mug' (don't deny it, it's one of your favourite expressions, 'classy mug' and 'squeaky-clean arse', Half Pint and Jeremy have now adopted them, too), and if by that you mean he's not like us, then just look at us. What the hell are we like?"

Sentences directly plugged into Marie-Colbert's neocortex.

"I need a man and a life that really are something, Benjamin.

72

That's my streak of originality, my break with family traditions . . . because when it comes to traditions (you know I don't want to hurt you) what you call our 'tribe' is a case in point. Rampant originality, that's our tradition."

Or else, in a more feminine tone:

"What would a woman's existence be like if she didn't bring her man to life to a certain degree? There are many women behind any successful man. Take you, for instance. Whatever people say, you're not a complete failure. And you needed Louna, Clara, Yasmina, Julie, Queen Zabo and me to get you where you are. Even mum contributed. See how vital women are? Grant Marie-Colbert this chance, Benjamin, let me bring him to life."

To which she added the unassailable:

"And grant me the right to get it wrong. I can make mistakes, just like everyone else. Do you want to know what mum dreamt of when she was young?"

There, I must admit, she'd flummoxed me.

"Look what I found in her tabernacle."

Mum's "tabernacle" was all we had left of her when she was off living her love life. A wicker box closed with a raffia knot, which Thérèse had apparently broken into. From it, she produced a cube-shaped hardback. To judge from the state of the cover and the publication date, mum must have inherited it from her own mother: *Woman, the Doctor of the House. Practical Advice for Newly Weds.* (Thus the title.) *Lady Doctor Anna Fischer.* (The authoress.) *Of the University of Zurich.* (Zurich again!) *The Popular Press, 1934.*

"Shall I read you a few extracts? Just the ones mum under-lined . . . Listen, Benjamin, listen to what mum dreamt of when she was my age:

"*Bodily intimacy between healthy and moral persons should take place only when there is a true feeling of love.*"

Mum underlined "bodily", "moral" and "true feeling of love".

"*If the man lacks respect for his spouse in many households, then this is because she herself lacks modesty and dignity.*"

In the margin: "How true" with a double exclamation mark: "!!" (Mum!)

"'*What is the basis for lasting happiness in a marriage?*' the author wonders. '*The spouses' moderation,*' she answers at once."

'Oh yes!' mum had pencilled in. Thérèse pointed at this 'yes' with a triumphant index finger. So, during her youth, mum had been tempted by moderation. Incredible. But by a particular sort of moderation, as was shown in the next sentence that had been underlined twice:

"*As regards conjugal relations, moderation consists in having them as seldom as possible, no more than once or twice a month.*"

Once or twice a month? . . . Mum? . . . Was that likely?

Thérèse then concluded with passion in her eyes:

"Why stop me from trying to make mum's dream come true, Benjamin? Where she failed, I can succeed. She'll be proud of me."

That's when I gave up the fight. Firstly, because there had been no hint of irony in Thérèse's delivery. Secondly, because if mum, that serial lover, had once dreamt of having once-monthly intercourse, then the field of love was so unpredictable that no-one could give anyone the slightest word of advice.

Christ knows why, but I finally nodded off thinking over the last extract from *Woman, the Doctor of the House*, which concerned hair care: "*Rather than fortifying the scalp, frequent visits to the barber destroy the hair's vitality. They may even be the main reason*

74

why the male sex often becomes bald." (Mum had underlined 'the male sex' then added a question mark.) I drifted off dreaming of a Marie-Colbert whose hair was so long and thick that Thérèse rolled it into Rasta dreadlocks.

Chapter 10

"CAN I HAVE my bed back?"

Someone asked me this question in the pit of my sleep.

"Benjamin, can I have my bed back?"

Someone I knew.

"Wake up, Ben, I need to sleep. Come on!"

Someone who was shaking me violently.

When I opened my eyes, Thérèse was there in front of me. When I opened my mouth, she did the talking:

"No, you're not dreaming. I'm back. The honeymoon's over. Now give me my bed back. I've got to sleep."

I backed out of the bedroom. Thérèse slipped between the sheets and turned towards the wall.

"We'll talk later."

Apart from Thérèse, the only other person in the hardware shop was Julie. Louna was on duty for three days at the hospital, Clara had gone to relieve Gervaise at Passion Fruit, and the rest were somewhere or other. Julie was filing Roberval data which was scattered across the tribal table.

"Don't ask me, Benjamin. You know as much as I do. She just

turned up and didn't say a word to me. Do you want some coffee?"

"Make it a strong one."

(Married on Saturday, back to base camp on Monday . . .)

"What's the time?"

"Nine thirty."

(. . . back at half past nine on Monday morning.)

Julie let the froth rise twice to the rim of the Turkish coffee pot.

"And promise me you won't start acting the avenging brother until you've looked into the whole business properly."

But this business was hard to look into. Thérèse slept all day. In the evening, when the store had filled again, the order was given to walk on cat's paws and gag the little ones. When Thérèse at last resurfaced at about nine (pm) – we'd kept her dinner warm in the oven, but she didn't touch it – she crossed the hardware shop staring straight in front of her. She just said:

"I'm going to put out Yemanja and pick up a few things."

Not even Jeremy asked her any questions.

Then she left.

Fine.

I asked:

"You coming, Julius?"

Julius the Dog never refused.

What's more, it was time for him to add to the monument he was piling up in honour of Martin Lejoli.

So out we went.

"I'm going to put out Yemanja." Which meant, when decoded, that the marriage had been consummated. Hence, loss of clairvoyance. No more use for Yemanja. Nothing to do but lock up the Bohemian caravan. So what had happened? And why so quickly? Had Marie-Colbert also gone back home? Something stopped me from finding out until I'd heard Thérèse's side of the story. I'd already had enough futile initiatives in this affair. All the same, Zurich . . . So just one day in that town was enough to wreck a relationship. And what a relationship!

It was one of those sultry evenings when, with all the windows open, Belleville becomes its own echo chamber. If I had listened carefully, I could have participated in all of the conversations within a square formed by Saint-Maur, Belleville, Pyrénées and Ménilmontant métro stations. Soon, these voices would converge on one subject and I would hear my own thoughts in my neigh-bourhoods' collective mind. "Thérèse *ierdjà*! Thérèse is back!" "*Wahed barka*, married for one day!" "Even her mother's never been that fast!" "*Wahed barka iaum*, just imagine it!" "On my life, if you'd told me, I'd never have believed it!" "*Po tian huang*! Never heard of such a thing!"

And so, as usual, I anticipated the future, while idly gazing at Julius, who was pushing.

Julius who was pushing . . .

That strange expression that dogs have when they push. It's always something that preoccupies them. They would prefer not to be seen, to look elsewhere, but the job requires all of their concentration. They need to achieve a perpendicular balance of the hindquarters and to calculate a precise trajectory, so as not to drop any on their paws or slump down into it. There are a large number of parameters to be borne in mind simultaneously. They would like to get it over with quickly and discreetly, but the busi-ness demands slow application. The forehead creases, the brows beetle. If there's one time dogs look as though they're thinking, a moment of total introspection, then it is when they're pushing.

Then, and only then, a dog's gaze becomes human. It even transcends us, if Martin Lejoli's horribly bland smile just above Julius was anything to go by. Complexity lay beneath, rigid ideas above. The fertile interlocking of varied needs below, monolithic obsession above, all of mankind's contradictions in Julius the Dog's eyes, a single motivation in the stare of candidate Lejoli. The thinker below, the predator above. And I felt scared. Not of the dog, of the man. I had an inkling of disaster. Once again, the copro-nimbus gathered over my head. I felt like running a mile. But one just cannot abandon one's dog in such a position.

"Get a move on, Julius!"

But Julius couldn't get a move on.

My fear swelled . . .

"No, Julius, no!"

. . . into a terror I knew only too well.

"For Christ's sake, not now!"

But Julius's epilepsy never picked the right moment. And what he was having, crouched there under that foul poster, with a visionary look in his eyes, lips pulled up in a grin, vampire fangs, Guernica tongue, long rising moan, was definitely an epileptic fit. His screams had soon drowned out Belleville's conversations. I rushed over as he slumped on to his side, still wailing as he fell, and I grabbed his tongue before he swallowed it. Then his wails stopped, but the terrible urgency that I read in his stare, that inspired supplication, what did it mean? What was wrong? What can you *see*, Julius? It made me do something I'd never done before. I left him there in the throes of his fit and ran where his eyes told me to go, and while I was running the air of Belleville caught fire. Immediately after the shock-wave of the explosion, I heard the bang, and I ran as fast as I could, though I knew it

79

was too late. And it was too late. When I got to Père-Lachaise cemetery, the Bohemian caravan was in flames, an inferno pointed up to the heavens, its heat warning off anyone who tried to approach it. "Thérèse!" I yelled, "Thérèse!" Then there was a second explosion and I saw a burning body being thrown out of the caravan, while its roof landed just next to me, and I kept on running, determined to dive in, to get Thérèse out of that hell hole, but something else fell on me and crushed me against the ground, a mass of muscles that was pinning me down on to the tarmac and protecting me against the burning debris, and I heard Simon the Berber's voice in my ear, whispering: "Stop, Ben, stop. There's nothing you can do!" Tears welled into my eyes and Thérèse's name stuck in my throat . . .

"Don't look!"

Simon's hand was pressing my cheek against the ground. All I could see were people running on the pavement outside Père-Lachaise. I heard cries.

"Shit, it's spreading to the cars!"

Simon grabbed hold of me. He ran, bent over me. I saw the flames emerge from the first petrol tank, then felt the shock-wave hit us.

"Fucking hell!"

Other people gathered round, dragging us to the shelter of the métro station. Only then did Simon let me go. So off I went again, up towards Thérèse.

"Come back, Ben!"

But all I could see was the tip of a tree catching fire and the flames lapping round the picture of a man on a revolving column of posters. The heat was pinning me down even more effectively than Simon's weight. The burning cars formed a barrier. The fire had now reached the taxi rank. One of the drivers, who had been trying to save his cab, abandoned it with its door open. He threw himself down on to the boulevard. His colleagues rushed towards him, wielding fire extinguishers. Then Simon caught up with me.

"Come on, Ben, come on!"

He pushed me and we crossed the street towards the wall of Père-Lachaise. Stumbling and sobbing out Thérèse's name, I was oblivious to the first siren.

"Watch out!"

The red truck just missed me, then hit a burning taxi and knocked it over on to its side. Men leapt out of the fire engine, diving into the blaze and forcing a way through with bright geysers of water, we were at the epicentre of converging sirens and redness, the dark blue of the police, the blinding chill of their flashing lights as they established a no-go area, but no matter how fast they worked, it was already too late, and all I could see was that charred body flying up into the air between the walls of Père-Lachaise and the shopfront of Letrou's Undertakers. The bare-chested man was shrivelling as the revolving column melted.

Then we had to deal with the arrival of the kids.

Jeremy first:

"Thérèse! Where's Thérèse? Was she in there?"

Then Half Pint, struck dumb, in a waking nightmare.

"Take the boys, Simon. Get them away from here!"

Half Pint and Jeremy rushed into Simon's arms. Clara was standing there motionless, holding her camera, but not daring to take a photo. Not this time.

"Follow them, Clara. Look after the boys!"
And Julie:
"Are you all right?"
"Julie, take them back home. All of them!"

Chapter 11

Until there was nothing left but the blackened carcasses of the vehicles, the paint swollen into boils, the plastic of the caravan melting on its chassis, the final flickers of blue flames at the base of the column on the sizzling tarmac, the wailing of the ambulance taking away the burnt cabby, the circle of ambulance men and coppers around the charred body. Which I wanted to see.

"Let him through. He's her brother!"

"You're her brother?"

But was I still the brother of that blackened thing with nothing left but its angles?

"She'd come to put out Yemanja."

"Yemanja?"

"Who's this bloke?"

"The victim's brother."

"Her name was Yemanja?"

Hadouch's voice:

"You OK, Ben? Can you hear me?"

"Take him to the wagon."

"He's in shock. We won't get a word out of him."

"Just take him!"

The cops ended up by getting me to say what I knew. They sent for Julie, Clara and the boys.

What about Verdun? And What An Angel? And Monsieur Malaussène? Who was looking after them?

"The little ones? Who's looking after the little ones?"

Hadouch told me that Yasmina was with them.

"Don't worry, Ben. My mother's put them all to bed up in your room. She's sleeping there too."

They got us to tell them everything that had happened since Thérèse's return. Separately. First in the paddy wagon, then at the station. It was so calm, those brief half-whispered questions, those fingers clicking on the computer keyboards, already the calm of bereavement, then finally our signatures at the bottom of the statements. Day was coming up as we left. It was five or maybe six in the morning. A dawn of petrol, plastic, tarmac, paint, dead flesh, a cold dawn of stagnant death. Amar, Hadouch, Rachida, Mo and Simon were waiting for us outside. I remember Rachida putting a shawl round Clara's shoulders. Then we went home.

On the way, Joseph Silistri, a friend of the tribe, caught up with us. Inspector (or Police Lieutenant, as they say now) Silistri.

"Can I have a word, Malaussène?"

He pulled me to one side while motioning to the others to keep moving. He was slightly out of breath.

"Sorry, I got here late. Titus has only just woken me up."

Inspector Titus was his other half, the second comedian in the double act. Titus and Silistri. The Tartar and the West Indian of Crime.

"We've been put in charge of the inquiry, Malaussène."

Already? How had they found out? I didn't want to know.

"Are you listening to me, Malaussène?"

Titus and Silistri were not part of the inner circle. They called me by my surname. Like bank colleagues who get on well. Silistri served me up the classic remark for this sort of situation:

"We'll get the bastards who did it, and no messing . . ."

So it wasn't an accident . . .

"You know . . ."

Silistri was trying to articulate his condolences.

"Our thoughts are with you all."

Which was probably true . . . But how can you comfort someone who's comforting you?

"Do you want Hélène to come round and see you?"

I really liked Hélène, Silistri's wife, but I already had a house full of mourners.

"Look . . . Given the state of the corpse . . . I mean of the body . . . that is, of Thérèse . . . her remains, in fact . . . you see, the . . ."

He was fighting though a morass of words.

"My superiors have decided . . ."

I really was there only in body. Words had lost their flesh, as had Thérèse, gone up in smoke, all of them. I was starting to wonder who these superiors were. Nuns maybe? Silistri's hair was glistening with sweat.

"So, I mean . . . it has been decided to continue the cremation."

I still didn't get it.

"You follow me, Malaussène? They've given the body to the cemetery, so they can finish the job in their crematorium."

He put his hand to his mouth. 'Finish the job' had just slipped out. He'd used up his humanity and professional banter

85

now had the upper hand. He was sorry. He apologised.

"I'm sorry."

Then he said:

"Normally speaking, we should have asked your permission, but Titus didn't want to bother you. So he signed for you. It should be over by now. Was he wrong to do that?"

No, no, Titus was right. We couldn't leave Thérèse like that. Nor bury her in such a state. I said thank you, very good, thank you, Titus was right, it was all for the best, thank you. And then I asked, on automatic pilot:

"Where is Titus?"

Silistri hesitated for a moment, then said:

"At the Robervals'."

Of course, with Marie-Colbert ... Of course, Titus had gone to break the news, to inform the widower ... Of course, it was only natural ...

"No, Malaussène. That's not really why ..."

No? Did Titus suspect Marie-Colbert? Was Marie-Colbert first on Titus's list?

"No, not that either."

Silistri looked me straight in the eyes for the first time.

"Roberval's been murdered too."

A copper's stare, impossible to say if he was questioning me, already accusing me or still thinking it over.

"He was found in his hallway. Thrown down the stairwell from the fourth floor. We were waiting for it to be morning before questioning Thérèse."

I said:

"Ah ..."

Then I went to join the others.

VI

In which what had to happen happens
or nearly

Chapter 12

Back at the hardware shop, we sat round the table while Julie made coffee.

"Jeremy, Half Pint, you'd better both get some sleep."

They shook their heads.

"Take them to bed, Clara."

Clara didn't budge.

"..."

They didn't even dare look at the bedroom door. I realised that they'd never sleep again.

"..."

"..."

Suddenly, I knew that I'd had it. I was fed up with this hardware shop, with Belleville, with the capital, with the air we breathe and the silence round the table. I was fed up with this tribe, with me and with being fed up. I said to myself that the solution was in fact easy. Thérèse had shown the way. She had once been among us, now she was no more. Simple. One moment you're here, the next you're gone.

"..."

"..."

Standing by the worktop, Julie was slicing bread then handing it to Clara to be toasted. A snip of the scissors sent the angle of a milk carton flying ... saucepan, gas, match ... and I was fed up with all that, too, fed up with reassuring gestures, with conventional reactions ...

" ... "

" ... "

"I'll be back."

I went up to our bedroom. Yasmina hadn't been able to face Thérèse's empty bed either. She'd taken Verdun and What An Angel from the kids' room and put them in our bed, with Monsieur Malaussène above them in a hammock. Sitting at the window, Yasmina was watching the sun come up. Just don't let her mention fate, that's all. Just so long as she doesn't tell me it was one of Allah's bright ideas.

She didn't. When she saw me she just said:

"*Ïa rabbi* ... (O my God ...)"

Then she opened her arms and without raising her voice:

"*Edji hena*, my little one."

I obeyed and went to her.

"*Bekä*, my son, *bekä*, you need to cry."

Which is what I tried to do as her arms wrapped round me. But nothing came. A complete drought. This went on until the arrival of daylight in all its innocent blueness, which rises up to us from the Place des Fêtes on cloudless mornings. That quivering beauty ... the renowned clearness of the Île de France ... I was fed up with that range of colours, too. Wasn't heaven just so delicate ... I was about to puke all over Yasmina's lap when someone knocked on the door.

Which then opened.

It was Jeremy.

"Ben . . . come here."

A wrecked Jeremy. As rigid as a picture of terror. Who was repeating, but without managing to raise his voice:

"Come on! Quickly!"

We were in one of those landscapes where anything could happen, where additional sorrows and catastrophes provoke a feeling of almost calm curiosity. Whatever next? And Jeremy standing there, pleading with me with his haggard voice:

"Come on . . ."

"*Mat yallah*, my son," said Yasmina. "Go . . ."

I stood up. I followed Jeremy.

He was going downstairs as though he was afraid of what he'd find at the bottom.

Downstairs, we found the same petrified tribe sitting in front of untouched bowls of white coffee. All of their stares were converging at the end of the table. Two men were standing there against the light. Two granite forms blocking out the morning sunshine. We couldn't see their faces. They'd placed an Easter egg on the table in front of them. They were waiting.

An Easter egg . . .

That was the first thing that struck me. A sort of large, pitch-black egg glinting metallically. A sinister, futurist egg. Laid by a steel pterodactyl. The profound silence in the room seemed to emanate from this egg. I jumped when one of the men spoke to me:

"Monsieur Malaussène?"

I answered yes.

The second pointed at the egg as though he was kneeling in front of a ciborium.

91

"The ashes of Mademoiselle, your sister."

Before the table had had time to absorb the shock, the first one started into the introductions:

"Messieurs Ballard and Fromonteux, from Letrou Limited."

Yes, yes of course ... Père-Lachaise had finished the job and passed the parcel to Letrou Ltd ... An inevitable progression ... The normal order of events ... Quite natural ... Thérèse's return home, that was all ... I thought with horror that the urn must still be warm. But an even deeper horror reminded me that there's nothing colder than cold ashes ... The utter coldness of ashes ... Like a palpable memory ... Not exactly of cold itself ... More of the absolute absence of warmth.

"Allow us to express our deepest sympathy."

"To you and to your family."

"From us personally and also from our company."

Ballard and Fromonteux spoke with the same voice. I stammered out a vague 'thank you'. They presumably took it for a conversational gambit, for they abruptly came to life.

"Does this model suit you?" asked Ballard or Fromonteux.

"If not," Fromonteux or Ballard went on, "our firm has an extremely wide range ..."

I heard an attaché case click open and, before we'd had time to make the slightest move, we found ourselves face to face with a batch of photos spread out around Thérèse's egg. Competing urns. Ballard or Fromonteux had dealt his pack with the same dexterity as Thérèse had once used with her tarot cards.

"As you can see for yourselves, funeral urns are moving with the times."

"It was high time the product had a fresh image."

"Our company has gone to great lengths."

"The dead also deserve diversity."

"Especially if kept at home."

"A variety of shapes and materials."

They were a real double act. With faultless timing. While Ballard or Fromonteux was talking, Fromonteux or Ballard went round the table placing a photo in front of each of us: urns shaped like a flower in full bloom, like a plump apple, an open book, childish urns with cherubic faces, a piggy-bank urn, to be broken open if we decided to spend Thérèse ... they even supplied the hammer.

"On special offer till October!"

"One thousand six hundred francs, plus VAT, mallet included . . ."

"Or one thousand nine hundred and thirty-six francs with the VAT . . ."

"Or two hundred and ninety-seven euros eighty-five cents . . ."

"Made of terracotta or porcelain . . ."

"In three interest-free monthly payments."

"Or this model, incrusted with Brazilian rubies . . ."

"Which of course represents rather a greater outlay . . ."

We were all totally flabbergasted, and I could see Julie's eyes silently screaming at me "Do something!", especially now that Half Pint had picked up one of the snaps. In my mind's eye, I could just see him declaring which one he liked best, then Jeremy's inevitable veto, followed by the usual fight with the two of them ripping each other to shreds in front of Thérèse's ashes.

Julie was right. I had to avoid that.

I quietened down my grief, I withdrew inside myself, I concentrated as much as I could and then, for the first time in my life, in my innermost self I openly begged for supernatural intervention.

The heavens heard my call.

And answered me.

Answered! Me!

Me! An habitual sinner, a terrible blasphemer, driven to the end of my faithless tether . . . Heaven answered my prayer!

At the very second Half Pint was about to open his mouth, a different voice echoed through the hardware shop. A voice that came from nowhere and was screeching one word:

"Yeeess . . ."

An angelic voice, languidly swooping around us:

"Oh, yeeeessss . . ."

His eyes agape behind his rose-tinted glasses, Half Pint dropped the photo. Everyone raised their heads. It was now Ballard and Fromonteux's turn to play at salt statues.

"Yes!" the voice was repeating in a hungry panting. "Yes! Yes! Yes! Yes! . . ."

A feminine angel, no doubt, a superbly female angel in full agreement with the joy of existence.

"Yeeeeeeeessssssssss!"

Who, having expanded this scream of pleasure to the full, curled up in a satisfied sigh, as though pulling the blankets over her.

Silence.

All the tribe's faces had turned towards the bedroom door.

A radiant Yasmina was rushing downstairs, peering all around.

"*Sema? Sema?*" she cried. "Did you hear that?"

I spun round.

I also stared at the door.

My fingers came to rest on the door handle.

I slowly opened it.

And yes . . .

Oh yes . . .

"..."

"..."

"..."

Thérèse was in her bed.

She was sleeping like a log.

No-one said a word.

While we still had our minds on the flashing grin of that charred thing or this UFO which had touched down on the dinner table, this phenomenon left us speechless. Even somewhat panicked, to judge from Ballard and Fromonteux's waxy complexions. They thought they'd seen it all, but this was certainly the first time they'd witnessed a resurrection. In retrospect, I wouldn't say that it was the miracle that amazed me most. With Thérèse, something of the sort was bound to happen sooner or later. No, that wasn't the most extraordinary part. The real surprise lay elsewhere. Thérèse, our terribly prudish Thérèse, who Jeremy reckoned was born in a cosmonaut's spacesuit, was naked! She was naked in bed for the first time in her life. And the rumpled sheets she'd carelessly pulled over her did nothing to hide her nudity, but rather accentuated its splendour. Because something else had happened, too. Thérèse had lost her angles! It was our Thérèse, no doubt about that, and yet not our Thérèse. A graciously curvaceous Thérèse, with dishevelled hair, drooping arms, smooth diaphanous skin and a fulfilled smile on her almost rosy face. The same old Thérèse, and yet a Thérèse that had suddenly been liberated, pumped full of hot blood which was beating just under her skin, a Thérèse who'd awoken to her true self after some mysterious journey.

"She looks like mum," Half Pint whispered.

Exactly.

"*Nâmet*," Yasmina murmured.

That was true, too. '*Nâmet*', it looked as though Thérèse was dreaming.

"But we aren't dreaming," Hadouch grumbled.

"Isn't it about time we started?" Rachida purred, wrapping her arms round him.

When Hadouch and Rachida were on their way out, something else happened. Thérèse's body started convulsing. Firstly with slight twitches, as though her skin was being ruffled by the breeze, then a series of spasms, one after another until Thérèse's entire body was trembling like a thing possessed, but without disturbing either her smile or her slumbers. A quivering beatitude that froze our blood. Even more terrifying than the classic image of a woman's twisted body being toyed at by the devil. I think we all took a step backwards. Thérèse was now jolting from head to foot, which made her sheets slip off, thus revealing her in her new splendour. No-one dared cover her. We stared at her with a mixture of horror and delight, as though some occult power was about to send us a message embossed on that marvellous flesh. A real b-movie, in fact, but one that was clearly delighting Thérèse. Then we heard knocking. Dull blows that were vibrating through the house. Coming up from the pit. A poltergeist was beating in time with Thérèse, who was still asleep and quivering more and more. Those taps on the floorboards, the scraping of bed legs, stifled moans, then that familiar smell . . .

The penny dropped.

I crouched down.

I looked under the bed.

"That's enough, Julius, come out from under there!"

Julius the Dog stopped scratching at once. He squeezed his

pudgy frame out. He, too, looked as though he'd risen from the dead. Not a trace of yesterday's fit. A slightly stronger stench, perhaps, and a perplexed glint in his eyes . . . Added humanity.

We did all we could to comfort Ballard and Fromonteux. Some coffee revived their spirits a little. They went back to Paris with a God-given mission: to find, among its seven million inhabitants, the grieving family which was waiting for their Easter egg. We'd given a meaning to their existences.

All the beds in the hardware shop were now occupied. Julie and I had regained our territory. We were slowly resurfacing when something crossed my mind:

"Julie, you did say 'condom'?"

"I beg your pardon?"

"You told me that Marie-Colbert looked like he always screwed with a condom, AIDS regardless."

"That's right."

"Well, you were wrong."

"Oh yes?"

"Thérèse's pregnant."

"How? Just like that?"

"A hundred to one says she is."

To which I added, more dead than alive:

"It's all coming true, Julie. Everything I predicted is coming true. Point by point. Marie-Colbert is dead. Thérèse is pregnant. You can call me every name in the book if you like, but I swear to you it's going to hit me. I know it is. It's right over me now. End of the dramatic build-up. In less than twenty-four hours' time, I'll be helping the police with their inquiries."

Chapter 13

JULIE DIDN'T CALL me any names. Instead, when Thérèse finally woke up, she helped me quiz her. The answers we got were extremely light-hearted:

"What do you expect me to say? Benjamin was quite simply right. Marie-Colbert was only after my clairvoyance. On Sunday morning, after our wedding night – which was no great shakes by the way – when I told my husband that my soothsaying days were over, I saw his face drop and so I left. That's all."

She trotted all this out merrily while dunking a slice of bread and bilberry jam into a bowl of milk. Her stare was candid, her chewing rapacious and her hand already reaching out for another slice. Thérèse was eating for two, tucking into a double breakfast, obviously pregnant with a ravenous squatter.

"You walked out just like that?" Julie asked. "Without waiting for confirmation? Without him throwing you out?"

Thérèse raised her eyes heavenward.

"Juuuuulie, I might not be a medium any more but I'm no sucker. I saw the expression on his face, I'm telling you! You know what men are like. If there's one thing they expect from us, it's for us to give them the courage to chuck us out. I got going at once, that's all. I waited for the night train then slipped back. Isn't there any more butter, Benjamin? Is this all that's left?"

Julie pressed her for more information. A detailed account of the honeymoon, for instance.

"Why?" Thérèse asked, while reaching out both hands towards the butter I'd brought her. "Who cares? That's all water under the bridge!"

"I just want to know what it's like," Julie insisted in the same merry tone. "This character here's never taken me away on a honeymoon."

She nodded towards me.

"You're not missing much!" Thérèse said while buttering her bread.

Then she told us that, as soon as they left Saint-Philippe-du-Roule, had got into that legendary ambulance and driven round the corner of La Boétie-George V, the newly weds dived into a taxi, then jumped into an aeroplane which dropped them off at a Bahnhofstrasse suite in Zurich, which was about as big as a runway.

"A hotel specially for 'squeaky-clean arseholes', Benjamin. Marble everywhere, impeccable service, two bathrooms and twin beds in the bridal suite, where champagne was awaiting us along with two dolled-up chambermaids and two copies of the management's congratulations. It was all just perfect. I thought of you, little brother. You'd have hated it."

So why was she in such a good mood? Why this sudden glibness? Who was this Thérèse? And how were we going to break the news of Marie-Colbert's death to her?

"And then?" Julie asked.

"Then, Marie-Colbert being Marie-Colbert, work being work

99

and responsibilities being what they are, both telephones rang and reception announced that the person we were expecting had arrived."

"You were expecting someone?"

"Someone in a suit and tie with a pile of papers we had to sign, who I certainly wasn't expecting. Marie-Colbert introduced me to Monsieur Altmayer, the treasurer of our association and then we got down to work. Marie-Colbert signed, I signed, then Monsieur Altmayer checked and signed. The papers circulated from right to left. It took us a good hour."

"And what were you signing exactly?"

Her smile was at once sensual and innocent (a bare-foot smile, Brigitte Bardot in one of her early films).

"As for that . . . you'll have to ask Marie-Colbert. I left him with two suitcases full of documents. You wouldn't fry me a couple of eggs, would you, Benjamin? I'm starving!"

Twins! She was brewing up twins for us! I thought again about what Half Pint had said. That joyous hunger and that carefree avidity were exactly like mum when she'd just dumped a progenitor. Marie-Colbert had twinned her!

"And then?" Julie asked.

"And then! And then! Have you got one-track minds, or what? And then we enter into the realm of privacy! What do you want to know? If I ripped his trousers off? If I raped him there and then? Well, I should have. But it was dinner time and this was not the sort of restaurant where a bride can drag her husband under the table . . . nor the sort of husband, for that matter."

The whites of the eggs were beginning to bubble up in the pan when she came out with what was, all things considered, the strangest part of her tale.

"Actually, as regards the wedding night, something really weird happened . . ."

I turned round, holding the pan by its handle.

"I'd like your opinion about this, Julie."

Julie raised her eyebrows in anticipation.

"He used a condom," Thérèse proclaimed.

My certitudes crumbled. The pan handle was still in my grip.

"Is that normal?" Thérèse asked. "On a wedding night, I mean? Does it often happen? With a girl you know is a virgin?"

Julie stammered out an answer from which it emerged that no, or else yes, sometimes maybe, that she wasn't a specialist in wedding nights, but that, who knows, given the present situation, perhaps Marie-Colbert wasn't sure about himself, on the other hand . . .

"When I think about it now," Thérèse butted in, "I reckon it was that which made me take the night train."

All this in the same mood of jollity, while the eggs were crackling in the pan. She was so radiant that we hesitated before telling her about the blaze in her caravan. Even that didn't unduly bother her.

"Really?"

She shook her head.

"The day before yesterday, I'd have told you it was destined."

My Thérèse had become armour-plated. Not the slightest chink in that steel case of jollity. I asked:

"What did you do last night, when you went out?"

"What I told you. I went to put out Yemanja."

"Were you alone in the caravan?"

"Of course I was! Everyone knows I've lost my gift."

"Did you leave anything switched on? A heater? A light bulb? A gas stove?"

"In this weather? It's summer, Benjamin. No, I threw everything I wanted to keep into a bag then left the door open on my way out, in case anyone wanted to sleep there. That's all."

We had to inform her that someone, a woman, had been burnt to death there.

This did cause a short break in her enthusiasm. Then she said:

"Well, I'd better go along to the police station and tell them that it wasn't me."

She got up to do so. I grabbed her by the wrist. I wanted to tell her Marie-Colbert was dead, but then a question occurred to me:

"Where did you go after putting out Yemanja?"

"I went for a stroll."

"Where exactly?"

Because it was this stroll that had obviously transformed her. On coming back from Zurich, she'd been in a terrible state. A beaten dog looking for its basket . . . Rolling over to face the wall . . . A zombie when she woke up . . . Misery on automatic pilot crossing the hardware shop to go and put out Yemanja . . .

Julie backed me up:

"Answer, will you, Thérèse? Where did you go after the caravan?"

She looked at us, first me, then Julie:

"What's eating the two of you? Am I under surveillance? A married woman? It's too late now! You should have spent more time watching the adolescent! With all her astrological bullshit . . ."

I must have looked a bit off colour, because she treated me to a peal of her new laughter and brushed her hand through my hair. Then she got to her feet again.

"I'm only teasing you, Ben . . . Look, I've got to talk to the police."

As she was leaving the hardware shop, Black Mo and Simon

the Berber sprang up from nowhere and stood either side of her. Then Hadouch appeared.

"We're going with her, Ben, OK? After all, someone maybe tried to murder her last night."

"I'm coming too," Julie said.

Some atmospheres are unmistakable. Things were piling up over me, closing in around me, the knot was tightening and I was in the middle. Thérèse might not be pregnant, but Marie-Colbert had definitely been murdered and disaster was at my doorstep. It was going to materialise in the shape of a paddy wagon and a pair of chrome-plated handcuffs. I'd been squirming around for weeks in vain. It was imminent. I felt almost relieved. As I was alone, I went up to our bedroom to prepare my convict's bag. Once packed, I dropped into Azzouz's shop to pick up the books that Queen Zabo and Loussa de Casamance had recommended.

"I haven't received them all yet, Ben. Is it that urgent?"

"I'll send you my new address so you can post them on to me."

Azzouz filled my rucksack.

"So, you're moving, are you, Ben? You're leaving Belleville? Has it gone too upmarket for you?"

"I'm taking a holiday, Azzouz."

He glanced at the titles one by one, before cramming them into my bag.

"Where, in a monastery? Very with it!"

I felt like having a last couscous. I first thought of the Koutoubia, but I couldn't stand the idea of confronting Amar, Yasmina and Old Sole with their farewell stares. So I headed off to the Deux Rives and sat at the round table where Rachida and I had discussed the evils of astrology. I ordered a makfoul, which I ate amid Areski's peaceful silence.

After which, I decided to take a stroll round Belleville with a disposable camera. I snapped whatever I came across, with no choice or discrimination. Memories are the fruit of chance. Only tricksters have ordered recollections.

Then I set off back home with the firm intention of loving Julie once more and for all time. But I realised that they weren't going to give me the chance. A police car was parked outside the hardware shop. Three plain-clothes coppers were waiting for me in front of the door. I recognised Titus and Silistri. I supposed that, given how well we got on, they were not here for the kill. I'd never seen the third one before. After explaining that their visit was to do with Marie-Colbert's death, Silistri introduced us.

Here we go, I said to myself.

"Deputy Public Prosecutor Jual," Silistri said.

Deputy Public Prosecutor Jual silently nodded.

"He'll be representing the Public Prosecutor's office during our inquiries," Titus explained to cover his embarrassment.

"The victim was an important figure," Silistri added.

With a frown, Deputy Public Prosecutor Jual made them understand that they were talking too much.

I almost said that I'd been expecting them, "just a second, I'll go and fetch my bag", but I didn't want to spoil their fun. I hunted for the typical thing one says in such circumstances and found it:

"How can I help you?"

"Your sister Thérèse is under arrest, Monsieur Malaussène," Deputy Public Prosecutor Jual proclaimed.

"Is she here?" Silistri asked.

They read in my eyes that she was there all right, just behind them. She was on her way back from the station. She was jauntily crossing the road between her bodyguards.

"She was seen last night at the scene of the crime," Titus whispered in my ear after the other two had turned round. "Seen and recognised. It's the telly's fault once again. Sorry, Malaussène, really I am. I would almost have preferred it to be you."

VII

Of marriage as a joint estate

Chapter 14

THEY HANDCUFFED HER and took her away before I could speak to her. I stepped towards her, but Titus held me back.

"She no longer has the right to communicate with you, Malaussène. It's more serious than you think."

Then Titus dived into the car, which pulled off.

I saw Thérèse one last time through the rear window between Silistri and Deputy Public Prosecutor Jual. Despite the handcuffs, she managed to waggle an index finger at me to signify "no", while pointing at herself with the other one. Maybe she meant "it wasn't me", or else "don't worry about me", especially since her eyes and mouth were still smiling, as though the three of them were taking her to drink orangeade on the banks of the Marne.

And I stood there.

With my rucksack full of books.

A complete twot . . .

So ashamed of myself . . .

So absolutely pathetic . . .

My first reflex was to leave Hadouch, Mo, Simon and Julie rooted there on the pavement, bomb up to our bedroom, unpack my bag at full speed, put away my stuff with the rapidity of a hamster stashing its droppings under a rug and throw my ruck-sack into the dirty-linen basket. All this ridiculous dissimulation made me feel even more ashamed, just look at yourself, just look at yourself, you creeping piece of shit, hiding away the traces of your screaming paranoia instead of worrying about Thérèse, about what's happening to Thérèse, about what Thérèse must have done to get handcuffed in front of you like that – handcuffed! in front of you! Thérèse! – and there's this wanker tidying his room so as not to be seen for what he is, get the books out of the laundry basket at least, how are you going to explain to Julie what John of the Cross is doing amid the dirty socks? Get them out of there, stuff them under the bed, they're winter reading, or some-thing like that, but why was she looking so radiant, is murdering your husband the day after your wedding night that much of a turn-on? Crushed in the stairwell, for Christ's sake, defenestrated in fact, thrown from a great height, pushed into the void, no it wasn't Thérèse, no, of course, it can't have been Thérèse, so what the hell was she doing there, that night on Rue Quincampoix, while I thought she was being burnt to death in her caravan, and so jolly with it the next day, so flippant about her Helvetic honeymoon and Titus with his "it's more serious than you think"! But I'm ready to imagine anything, I am, except Thérèse grabbing a Grade One Public Auditor by his heels – even if he were her husband – then chucking him over the banister rail of his town house before coming back home in delight after seeing – and hearing, of course – his body hit the ancestral marble sixty feet below, no it wasn't Thérèse, unless our sisters aren't our sisters, but what, Malaussène, are you tidying up your room for like a dickhead instead of going downstairs and drawing up a battle plan with the others, who do you take yourself for? Look at yourself, you're making your bed, Malaussène, nice and neat, like a good soldier, funny how the subconscious takes over, and you're carefully filing away the books on your shelves, the novels with the novels, poetry, plays, social sciences, philosophy, religion and Robert Antelme's *L'Espèce Humaine*, where to put *L'Espèce Humaine*? That's a real problem of civilisation, that is, where to file away a book like *L'Espèce Humaine* in a twentieth-century bookcase? In which section? For each century, ladies and gentlemen, has its speciality, that's what our children learn at school in strict chronological order: poetry for the sixteenth century, plays for the seventeenth, the Enlightenment in the eighteenth, novels in the nineteenth, then what about the twentieth? What's the twentieth century's speciality? *Concentration Camp Literature*, ladies and gentlemen, a marvellous section if you want to forget nothing, to follow current affairs, and to foresee what's coming next . . .

Deputy Public Prosecutor Jual, Thérèse, Titus and Silistri came back that afternoon, escorted by a squad of uniformed officers. DPP Jual brandished a search warrant covered with rubber stamps and ordered us to keep our distance from the still-handcuffed Thérèse. We all stayed downstairs, sitting round the table under the watchful eye of a bitch of a copperesse and a white truncheon that was dying for a bit of action. The rest looked for something. They looked everywhere, in the kids' bedroom, the kitchen cupboards, the washing machine, the toilet cistern, the mattresses, everywhere. I heard my books come tumbling down from the shelves and thought of all the time I'd wasted. They knocked on the walls, ceilings, floors and dug into everything that sounded hollow. They violated mum's tabernacle. To judge from the copperesse's stare, they'd have ripped Julius the Dog in half if they thought he was hiding anything of interest. (All the same, what about those girls on the force now, the way their schooling turns out . . . see how the uniform chills their eyes and stiffens their jaws one or two degrees more than their male colleagues, and the prettier they are, the more they turn into stalagmites, it's a real tragedy the way they're trained up, the social services ought to be doing something about it . . .) As for Thérèse, just look at her, the honeymoon killer, the spousicide, just look at her grace, that liberty of movement, the relaxed way she walks in front of the investigators, leading them from room to room discreetly as though she was letting out our hardware shop as a holiday home, as though she was talking up our place's market price, it's handiness for big families, Christ, what happened to her last night? What caused this transformation? Tell me who liberated you so completely, Thérèse! But she said nothing, not to the cops, and not to us, just the odd pout that was supposed to reassure us, "don't panic, don't fret about me, I'll be fine", until they left empty-handed, their faces ashen, they'd drawn a blank, found nothing, what a let-down.

While they were passing in front of me, I couldn't resist it, I leapt towards our handcuffed Thérèse, but Police Lieutenant Titus intervened in a dryly professional manner, with thumbs in the palms of my hands and a backward twist of the wrists.

"Sit down!"

By the time I'd recovered, the hardware shop's door had swung shut. I was sitting there, among my loved ones, my fists clenched, ready to kill. Then I felt something in my right hand. I opened it. A piece of paper fluttered down on to the table. I unfolded it. Titus had written just one word on it: "Gervaise".

*

If I remind you that, during another lifetime, Gervaise used to work as an investigator with Lieutenants Titus and Silistri, and that Titus and Silistri had been Gervaise's guardian angels, then you can easily decode Inspector Titus's message: "Contact Gervaise". That was Titus's advice. "Gervaise knows". Such was my deduction.

I stood up.

Julie stopped me.

"How many plain-clothes cops do you think are waiting outside to trail you?"

Hadouch agreed:

"We're trapped here. We can't even go take a leak."

Silence.

"What if we sent Rachida?" Simon suggested.

Hadouch didn't look at all keen.

But the idea appealed to Black Mo, too.

"The coppers don't know Rachida. She leaves work. She goes and sees Gervaise. And there we are."

No, Hadouch was dead set against.

"She'll just get grilled when she comes back."

Hadouch didn't want his new darling to get caught up in this business. We had to find another way to contact Gervaise.

"How about phoning her?"

No, the subject was too serious for telephony. Anyway, our phone was almost certainly being tapped.

"Right, so what shall we do, then?"

That's where I took over. I pointed out that Sister Gervaise ran an honourable institution, to which we had entrusted the care of our children, and that no policeman, be he uniformed or in mufti, in hiding or in the open, was going to stop me from carrying out my paternal duty, that I'd had it up to here with all this "victim-fixated paranoia" – yes, I definitely think I said "victim-fixated paranoia" – I was now on automatic pilot, entering my heroic phase, weaving a banner of concepts to brandish while launching my assault on the "Police State", and all on my own, if need be! If they let me come out with two or three more sentences of this calibre, then I'd bulldoze down the entire police headquarters so as to release Thérèse, even if it meant taking Deputy Public Prosecutor Jual hostage.

Julie must have sensed that this was an emergency, because she interrupted my gushings by opening her hands.

"All right, all right, no need to work yourself up into a state. Let's go, let's go . . ."

Chapter 15

SO HADOUCH, MO, Simon, Julie and I went to see Gervaise at Passion Fruit.

"It's quite handy, as a matter of fact," said Hadouch. "Rachida wanted to put her baby's name down anyway."

Simon raised an objection:

"But Rachida's kid isn't going to be a whorelet!"

"We'll ask her to make an exception."

"What An Angel and Monsieur Malaussène aren't whorelets either," Julie pointed out.

"That's not what I meant," Simon apologised.

There were so many plain-clothes coppers following us, and so many onlookers following them, with everyone marching along briskly, that we formed a minor demonstration. Belleville rising up against Pigalle.

But, when we got to Père-Lachaise métro, Belleville ran into Pigalle coming to meet it. Gervaise was calmly coming up the station steps. She had What An Angel in a sling and Monsieur Malaussène on her back. Clara was following her with two shopping bags and Verdun in tow. Jeremy and Half Pint brought up the rear.

Never count on Gervaise to up the dramatic tension. She just said:

"As you were late, we decided to take them home ourselves."

There was a moment's hesitation, then the demo did an about turn. I almost apologised to the police. The onlookers looked rather pissed off, as though we'd stopped them from seeing an episode of the story.

Gervaise pointed to Jeremy and Half Pint:

"Clara and I bumped into these two intellectuals on the way home."

Jeremy and Half Pint were both bent double under their satchels.

"Is Thérèse in?" Jeremy asked, dumping his load in the hallway of the hardware shop.

"Is she awake? Is she here?"

I closed the door. I looked at Jeremy. I said Thérèse was somewhere else.

"Where's that?" Half Pint asked.

I said we didn't know.

"There's no holding her since she got married!"

I said I thought so too.

"So who was the bird in the caravan?" Jeremy asked.

"Yes, who was it?" Half Pint echoed him.

"You're on duty," answered Gervaise, handing What An Angel and Monsieur Malaussène to Jeremy.

She pointed upstairs.

"The rest of us have things to discuss."

"Can I come?" Half Pint asked.

"What you can do is lay the table," Julie replied.

"With an extra place," Gervaise added. "I'm inviting myself to dinner."

"Plus another three," said Hadouch. "We're sticking aroun
as well."

"And we're fussy about the service," Simon pointed out.

"Too right," the Black concluded.

I followed the herd. We went up to our bedroom. Gervaise ha
a story for us.

A story which Inspector Silistri had told her over the phone.

An oral tradition, a tale she was supposed to relay to us.

A story we already knew well, apart from a few details:

The Geste of Roberval
Last count of that name
Part I: Love

IT STARTED ON an exotic note. A Belleville Cantonese,
named Zhao Bang, had just had his *I Ching* read by
Thérèse Malaussène. According to him, his wife had left
him, and he was dying of remorse, sorrow, shame, anger
and impotence. Loss of honour, of appetite, of sleep and of
dignity, constant whingeing, bottles of ginseng, aimlessness,
didn't know what he was about, or where he was going,
until a friend pointed him towards the Bohemian caravan
of a certain Thérèse Malaussène who told fortunes down
on Boulevard de Ménilmontant, between Père-Lachaise and
Letrou Undertakers, see where I mean? You should see her,
Zhao, I promise you, she's really something! "*Wo qu!*" (I'm
going!). Thérèse Malaussène received Zhao Bang, listened to
him, cast down her sticks, then reassured him: Ziba would
come back (Ziba being the foot-loose missus in question),
Ziba was maybe already home, yes, Zhao Bang should take

off back to his flat and have a look. So off Zhao Bang ran, Zhao Bang had a look, and then Zhao Bang returned with Ziba, for Thérèse Malaussène had been quite right, his adulterous lady had come back, Ziba was home!

First consequence: the Malaussène family ate Cantonese cuisine day and night until Verdun, Jeremy and Half Pint started a hunger strike to demand the return of couscous and gratin dauphinois.

"That's right. I remember now. I hadn't made the connection."

Second consequence: a fortnight later, a tall smooth stranger, worthy and upright in his three-piece suit, his well-rounded butt under the impeccable back-flaps of his jacket, was waiting for Thérèse Malaussène in the queue outside her Bohemian caravan. When it was his turn, he introduced himself, his name, title, position, Marie-Colbert de Roberval, nth Comte of that name, Councillor Grade One, and laid before Thérèse the astral data of a brother whose future was worrying him. Or so he said. And so it should. For the future in question had been hanged off a beam in his ancestral home two weeks before by his brother, Charles-Henri. Thérèse detected the lie and offered consolation. Marie-Colbert should stop fretting, his professional inquiries had had nothing to do with it, Charles-Henri's death was down to the stars and to love, for love kills us like a game of chance, with the knowledge that we can never go back and win what has been lost. This comforted Marie-Colbert a bit. And embarrassed him much more. He twisted his elegant fingers. He squirmed like a teenager. He clumsily asked if he could, if it would be all right, if in fact Thérèse would see him again. For a consultation? As often as he wanted, for the caravan was open from dawn to dusk. No, not for a consultation, in fact. In private. In as much privacy as possible. Why? "To do good," Marie-Colbert de Roberval replied. Good? Good. And not just for a neighbourhood in Paris, but on a global scale. Global? Yes, the entire planet, which so needs good being done to it, the poor thing.

End of Part One.

Gervaise paused.

"So that's how Roberval recruited Thérèse."

"Recruited her?"

"Yes, without her even noticing. Through the Cantonese couple."

The Geste of Roberval
Last count of that name
Part II: War

THÉRÈSE MALAUSSÈNE'S LIFE hardly changed. She carried on enlightening the future in her caravan. But new pilgrims had joined the old: same races, same languages, same variety, apparently the same clientele ... Except that Thérèse didn't sell the future to the newcomers, she secretly provided them with emergency supplies, drugs of all sorts, blankets, tents, clothes, infirmaries, operating theatres, school books, pencils, biros, rubbers, ambulances, seeds, farm tools, in fact everything that could be given in the name of life ...

Yes, yes, we know all that already. And so?

So, Thérèse followed the instructions of the now invisible

Marie-Colbert: this quantity for that person, that quantity for this one, according to scales and strange codes which Thérèse applied without understanding a word. For instance, 223,432 aspirin tablets, even if aspirins can be bought in bulk in the chemist shops of the third world. That precise figure, two hundred and twenty-three thousand four hundred and thirty-two aspirins, no more no less, should have given her pause for thought.

"Why?"

Gervaise looked at me. She hesitated. She finally dropped the story format and started into her exegesis.

The Geste of Roberval
Textual analysis

GERVAISE: Because if you replace each aspirin with an anti-personnel mine, Benjamin, then the figure becomes far more . . . eloquent.

ME: . . .

GERVAISE: And the biros with rocket launchers, and the suppositories with ground-to-air missiles, and the ambulances with machine-guns and boxes of staples with cases of ammunition . . .

ME: . . .

GERVAISE: . . .

ME: . . .

GERVAISE:

HADOUCH: So, in fact Thérèse was gun-running when she thought she was supplying medicines?

GERVAISE: And she received her cut in a Swiss bank on Bahnhofstrasse in Zurich.

JULIE: *Her* cut?

GERVAISE: Yes, in an account Marie-Colbert opened in her name.

OK, OK, the penny'd dropped. Thérèse Malaussène, or the perfect cover. Weapon smuggling based in the caravan of a tarot reader, who really thinks she's doing charity work. The money goes into a Swiss account, under her name. If the network gets uncovered, Councillor Roberval comes up smelling of roses. Thérèse Malaussène? Never heard of her. Zhao Bang? Who he? Ziba? Come again? Recruitment? Whatever do you mean?

So the wedding then? Why did he marry her?

ME: What about the wedding then? Why did he marry her?

GERVAISE: To get his money back. Roberval let the business run on as long as he saw fit. When he reckoned he'd earned enough and there was still no danger on the horizon, he married Thérèse, with a joint estate contract, and took her to Zurich to collect.

JULIE: And in the process gave himself the image of a perfect humanitarian.

GERVAISE: Exactly.

JULIE: They really are a model family.

Despite everything, there was an excited ring in Julie's voice. A buried smile. Gervaise had just given her the last chapter of her Roberval monograph, its crowning glory.

GERVAISE: ...

ME: ...

GERVAISE: In Zurich, Marie-Colbert took the entire sum out in cash. Two full suitcases. Large denomination dollar bills. That is what Deputy Public Prosecutor Jual was looking for this afternoon.

SIMON: Because they reckon Thérèse whacked her husband and legged it with his dosh?

GERVAISE: They suspect her of murder, and the money is missing.

God knows she made a good suspect! What was she doing that evening on Rue Quincampoix, holding a bag and running like a thing possessed towards a cab? As for a motive, they were legion: frustration, feeling of betrayal, revenge of good over evil, or just plain simple vengeance, the vengeance of the cheated wife . . .

GERVAISE: . . .

ME: . . .

GERVAISE: . . .

JULIE: . . .

HADOUCH: What was the name of the Cantonese head-hunter again?

GERVAISE: Zhao Bang.

Hadouch turned round. Mo and Simon got to their feet.

THE BLACK: Zhao Bang?

SIMON: Right.

They left. Gervaise listened to their footfalls die away on the staircase, then said:

"Still, there is just one point in Thérèse's favour."

Just one . . .

"The statement made by Altmayer, their Swiss intermediary."

ME: . . . ?

GERVAISE: He's an undercover cop, who infiltrated Roberval's network via the Swiss bank. According to him, Thérèse's completely innocent. In every sense of the term.

HADOUCH: A bit simple, you mean?

GERVAISE: When it comes to money, at least. When he saw her sign the papers to close the account without even reading them, without even noticing that money was involved, he realised that she had no idea what was going on. He says she was over the moon after her wedding, very excited, and in a hurry to get the formalities of her husband's charity work over and done with. He'll confirm this in court.

ME: That's better than nothing.

GERVAISE: There are just a couple of nagging details left.

The first was that Marie-Colbert had been found in his socks. But the Councillor Grade One was not the sort to wander round in his stockinged feet. Except with someone he knew, perhaps. A good thirty pairs of shoes in his wardrobe, and his corpse in socks. The killer was certainly known to him. First point. Secondly . . .

ME: . . .

GERVAISE: He had a plane ticket in his pocket. He was set to leave two hours later. Alone. To the Seychelles. Was he going to join someone there? A woman perhaps? Hence the idea that he was murdered from jealousy . . .

HADOUCH: If you've got a copper's imagination.

ME: Which gives them an extra motive.

GERVAISE (hesitating): There's one more thing. Strangely enough . . . he was smiling.

JULIE: What do you mean, he was smiling?

GERVAISE: He died with a smile on his face. He looked extremely merry in fact. You could see that he'd been killing himself.

ME: Like Thérèse ever since that night, is that what you mean?

GERVAISE: The fact is that, given the circumstances, the investigators don't understand the joy on the dead man's face, or Thérèse's jubilant mood. But that's not the strangest part . . .

Here, Gervaise hesitated for a moment. The discreet embarrassment of the awkward pause.

"Benjamin, I feel terrible asking you this, but do you think

Thérèse has been having an affair with a married man?"

We all gawped at one another. Thérèse? An affair? With a married man? A contradiction in terms! Gervaise shook her head:

"That's what I think, too, which is rather a pity."

"Why?"

"Because, when asked what she was doing at the time of the murder, she claims that she was making love. It's her only alibi."

"Who with?"

"She won't say. She says that someone's honour depends on her silence. And that's all they can get out of her. She's ready to spend her life behind bars to protect this person's honour, and is even delighted about the idea! Titus and Silistri are furious."

I've always been sensitive to silences. And the silence that had just descended on us was one of the tensest in my collection. I slowly turned round towards Hadouch. And Hadouch slowly opened his eyes with surprise. What? I suspected him? Him? With Thérèse? He'd been there when she was born!

I countered his stare. What? Suspect me of suspecting him? Me? Who'd always been his brother?

He groaned.

I looked daggers at him.

Business concluded.

Gervaise summed up:

"There we are. All you have to do now is find the married man Thérèse was making love with that night. You've got forty-eight hours. When the questioning's over, she's going to be up before the magistrates."

VIII

In which we search for the truth
without ducking the question of torture

Chapter 16

FINDING THE MAN Thérèse was laying while another was widowing her seemed easier said than done. I set about it the next morning, but without knowing where to start. Might it be another political passion? Another Roberval, whose great altitude meant that a man's honour was worth a woman's imprisonment?

"Such things happen," Julie said. "I'll try that angle. As for you, Benjamin, you take care of the others."

What others? Friends Thérèse might have gone to for shelter that night? Who? Marty, the family doctor who'd been treating her since she was born? Berthold the surgeon, who she worships because he resurrected me? Gervaise's Postel-Wagner, who delivered Monsieur Malaussène? Inspector Caregga, to whom I owe at least three lives? Would one of these irreproachable friends have made the most of the situation by . . . With Thérèse? No! Why not Loussa de Casamance while we were at it, or old Amar, or Rabbi Razon? And then, how to go about investigating? By phoning them up? "Hello, is that Marty? Hi, it's Malaussène. Tell me, you didn't shag my sister Thérèse on the night of Monday to Tuesday, by any chance? Yes, Monday night, do try and remember,

it's rather important . . . You didn't? You're sure about that? Fine."
Or else play the copper, and set the suspects against one another:
"Good evening, Berthold, Malaussène speaking. In your opinion,
who did Thérèse spend Monday night with?" No, I could just
imagine that distinguished sod's reply: "I'd check out Marty, if
I were you, Malaussène. Anyway, you know me, I'm as straight as
a die, and when it comes to the sack, my missus is worth fifteen
of your sisters. She's a real pro!"

No, I couldn't do that. Suspicion is not one of my strong suits.
If I found mankind in general to be suspect, I still trusted its
individual members.

And then, there was a major obstacle. To begin with, I was going
to have to convince them that Thérèse had slept with someone,
which was utterly incredible for anyone who knew her.

Our sister Louna, for instance, who I called while she was on
duty at the hospital:

"Thérèse? Making love? And loving it? Are you kidding,
Benjamin?"

Louna had easily accepted the rest of the tale: Thérèse's return
the day after her wedding, the exploding caravan, her arrival in
a warm urn and subsequent resurrection was all run-of-the-mill
Thérèse. Even Marie-Colbert's transformation into a gun-runner
didn't shock her, his tragic death and Thérèse's arrest all bore
the stamp of the Malaussène tribe, were just one further episode
in our family saga and nothing to drop the receiver about. But
Thérèse in bed with some bloke? No way.

"Christ, Louna, but that's what she's telling the police! And you
know she never lies."

"Maybe she's talking in parables."

"The only other alternative is that she murdered Marie-Colbert.

128

Louna, can you imagine Thérèse chucking Marie-Colbert over the banisters?"

"Thérèse is unimaginable, Benjamin."

"Thanks for your help . . ."

One of those pregnant pauses ensued, during which each party is thinking furiously.

"Anyway, who knows what Thérèse means by 'making love'?" Louna finally suggested. "You know her, as soon as sex comes up, she goes all metaphorical."

True enough. Only too true, in fact. Which widened the scope of the investigation even further.

"Sorry, Ben . . . I really can't help you. You know Thérèse never confides in me! Nor do you, for that matter!"

This sort of reproach from Louna never stops there, especially when she's fed up or pissed off with her husband.

"OK, Louna, we'll leave it there. Sorry I bothered you, you must be rushed off your feet and . . ."

"Listen to me before you hang up."

You don't escape so easily from the family quicksand. I sat down to hear out Louna's lament:

"OK, I'm listening."

"It'll be the first time you've ever listened to me!"

For some reason unknown to me, Louna had never really felt loved, and this lack greatly hampered her marital bliss with Laurent.

"Anyway, in this family, no-one's ever been able to confide in anyone else. Especially not in you, Benjamin. Always busy, or elsewhere, even when you're physically present. We've all had to make do, Clara with her camera, Thérèse with her stars, mum with her lovers, Half Pint with his nightmares, Jeremy with his anger, and me . . ."

Cast a pontoon over Louna's pit, I don't want to sink with her.

"Louna . . ."

"I know, I know, this is no time to start whingeing!"

"That's not what I meant!"

"Just as well. I'm in no mood for a whinge. I just wanted to give you some advice."

On the verge of tears. She hesitated. She sniffed. She swallowed. Then went for it:

"Theo's the only person who can help you, Benjamin. Theo's always been our confidant, even when we were kids. Theo's always listened to us, has always been available, even when he wasn't physically present. I can tell you now that, when you forbade us to go out, and when we did a bunk, it was Theo we told where we were going, in the unlikely event that you got worried, which you never did. Just think about it, who did Thérèse confide in when she met Marie-Colbert? In you? Who did she tell first? You?"

No, Theo. It was Theo, all right. "I'm the old agony aunt who hears everyone's unrepeatable secrets." Theo, of course! Why hadn't I thought of that? If Thérèse had slept with anyone other than Marie-Colbert, then Theo would have been told. Theo would be in the know!

Assuring Louna of my love and her brilliance, I gently hung up: You're a genius, Louna. Theo, of course. Then I ran to the métro, yelling that I was going to Theo's, that if "anyone asked for me", I was at Theo's, my old mate Theo's, he who, during all the years that I'd tried to knock some sense into that family of loonies, had tolerantly covered up their escapades, good old Theo, who'd forged for himself the reputation of an understanding uncle, while I'd picked up the image of the tyrannical big brother, Theo who caught on to everything while I heard nothing, such a good "listener" who was always "available" compared with that autistic big brother, uncle Theo who was so lucid that he'd been the first to give his blessing to Thérèse's marriage, so extraordinarily clairvoyant that he'd pitched Thérèse into bed with a gun smuggler, so highly perspicacious that he'd packed Thérèse off to make babies with a condom machine! And if uncle Theo had stage-managed all of that, then presumably he also knew what happened next, and I was dying to know what had happened next, Thérèse's second choice of hubby, the hard-hitting inseminator, the provider of instant comfort . . .

I leapt out at Rambuteau, I ran straight past the Pompidou Centre, with Julius the Dog barely able to keep up, at 3 Rue aux Ours I took the stairs four at a time, then I repeatedly hammered on the door until it opened.

When it did open, I grabbed Theo by his shoulders, I pinned him against the wall and bawled into his face the sentence I'd been chewing over ever since I'd left home:

"Where's the cunt who fucked Thérèse last night and is now leaving her to rot in the slammer?"

But Theo was in no state to reply. He even scared me and Julius a bit. There was Theo, pale, his eyes buried in their sockets, wobbling on his pins, scrawny, shattered and angular. He looked like Thérèse before her metamorphosis. So wasted away I nearly went out to fetch medical assistance. I released my grip. I asked:

"You all right, Theo?"

He slid down the wall without answering. He didn't even seem to recognise us. I stood him back up, propped him against the doorframe, then walked further into the flat, with Julius getting between my legs in fretful curiosity. Another voice drifted across to us:

"Who is it, sweetie pie?"

A voice that sounded like Theo looked . . . more of a last gasp than a voice, in fact. I looked round but couldn't see anything. The curtains were drawn and the blinds down. The external shutters added to the gloom, and the absurd thought occurred to me that night had been piling up there in that room for all eternity. That's when the stench hit me. A musky odour made of the same substance as that darkness. Not only could I not see anything, I couldn't even breathe. Or rather, the air I was breathing had already been recycled so many times before my arrival that it was suffocating me, in the midst of that night, full of an intimacy that wasn't mine . . . I'd been thrown into the pit of a stranger's womb!

"Theo, darling, come back to bed!"

Jesus . . .

No need to be psychic to guess who that unfamiliar voice belonged to . . . *"Two days and nights in Hervé's arms. Marie-Colbert insisted on inviting him over for a weekend in bed"* . . . Isn't that just like you, Malaussène? I thought to myself. Worrying about Theo's state of health, when he's been shagging himself senseless for the last two days with his new Mister Right! Two days and two nights that our friend here had been drawing his wages for a bridal gown, while the bride in question had narrowly avoided being burnt to death, had then been arrested, handcuffed, thrown in jail, while in the meantime being impregnated by an outsider.

I drew back the curtains, I rolled up the blinds (two long eyelids of mauve latex that fluttered their lashes at me as they rolled up), I opened the windows, I sent the shutters flying, Theo had got back into bed with Hervé, and the scene froze in the dazzling sunlight.

"Who's this?" Hervé asked, while shading his eyes. "A jealous ex?"

He didn't know how right he was. Seeing them there in bed, worn out by forty-eight hours' non-stop shagging, their matted hair glued against their gleaming brows, that inspired glow in the depths of their eye-sockets, their hearts beating in their temples, made me think of Julie ... and how badly I'd loved her since the copro-nimbus had formed over my head! So, yes, I was jealous. Jealous of the record these two thought they'd established, as though Julie and I were incapable of losing two stone in two days, so much weight that it felt as though our bodies weighed a ton! As though we couldn't scatter round the room ten times more clothes than we'd actually been wearing! As though we'd never cemented the sheets together with our pleasure and soaked the air with our essences! As though we had no intention of loving each other to death as well! As though the very thought of a different end had ever occurred to us ...

So, jealous I was of these two playmates and, while I'm at it, jealous of the pleasure that was teasing out Thérèse's smile, and jealous of that anonymous fucker who was hiding out someplace leaving my sister to sleep off all that voluptuousness in jail.

I threw a handful of clothes at Theo, then I looked round his kitchenette.

"Get dressed then answer my questions yes or no."

I put the Turkish coffeepot on to boil, resolved to make him drink through his ears if necessary and started my interrogation:

The two of them had been fucking like madmen for the last forty-eight hours, yes or no?

"Yes."

So Theo didn't know that Thérèse had been put behind bars?

"No."

Nor that she was pregnant?

"Pregnant! That quickly?" Theo exclaimed.

"But that's wonderful!" Hervé chipped in.

The sugar-saturated water began to boil in the coffeepot. I took a deep breath, then said as calmly as possible:

"Theo, answer yes or no and ask your friend here to keep out of it."

"You have to understand, Ben, babies are so important for us . . ."

I hit the roof . . . I told him I had other things on my mind, that Thérèse was in the slammer, that on the night of the murder she'd been shagging some dickhead who hadn't come forward, and since Theo'd always been our agony uncle he now had to put his thinking cap on and produce the name of the person who'd impregnated my sister, and quickly with it, so I could collar the bastard then kick his arse round to Deputy Public Prosecutor Jual's office so he could act out his part as an alibi. Clear?

He nodded.

"So shift your butt! You've only got half a day left before she's up before the beak!"

Chapter 17

I BOMBED BACK downstairs and grabbed a cab. I was in a hurry to get back to the hardware shop, just in case Thérèse had materialised there again during my absence. Julius the Dog knew the score. To be allowed into a taxi, he had to hide till I opened the door, at which point he then leapt in in front of me. When a cabby spots him before stopping, he puts his foot down and vanishes over the horizon as though he had his own conscience running after him. But if Julius succeeded, then we were sure to get the shortest, fastest and quietest ride home. No question of giving the customer the tourist route with His Pestilence in the back. And no complaints about the job, which isn't what it used to be, customers who think they know the best routes, women who drive like women, poofters who want to be able to get wed, A-rabs gobbling up the welfare state, Chinks colonising Belleville, no-one's safe at night and hurray for Martin Lejoli! Reciting this litany requires breath, and Julius the Dog is a magnificent deterrent.

Thérèse wasn't at home.

I made some coffee and called up Gervaise at Passion Fruit. Her news wasn't particularly reassuring. According to Silistri, Thérèse was slowly but surely becoming suspect number one. Not only did she refuse to reveal her alibi's name, but her excellent mood came over as being smug cynicism. Deputy Public Prosecutor Jual now even suspected her of setting fire to her own caravan.

"What?"

"That's what Silistri's just told me on the phone."

"Why would she have done that?"

"From jealousy, Benjamin. To wipe out a rival."

"A rival? What rival?"

That was the crux. The police had really screwed up when they cremated the corpse the other night. Everyone had been so sure it was Thérèse. So there was no way to identify the stiff any more. Except that, during their investigations into Marie-Colbert, Titus and Silistri had decided to question the sister-in-law, Charles-Henri's widow. And they hadn't been able to locate her. She'd vanished. Since yesterday.

"And you know what Thérèse says when asked if she suspected Marie-Colbert and his sister-in-law of having an affair?"

What did you say, Thérèse, for Christ's sake? What did you come out with this time?

"She says that she can't tell them anything, that if they were having an affair, then that was Marie-Colbert's and her business, that our private lives are our last haven, and that they shouldn't count on her to violate anybody's privacy."

Oh, Thérèse ... Thérèse ... Thérèse and her principles ... Thérèse and her right and wrong ... Who cares if you're right when getting grilled? Are the interrogatees there to teach the interrogators manners?

"Deputy Public Prosecutor Jual is almost certain that Thérèse made an appointment with her sister-in-law, burnt her alive then settled her score with Marie-Colbert."

"Which gives us two murders for the price of one."

"Yes, a double premeditated murder. Titus and Silistri are furious but powerless. They find Thérèse disconcerting, as though she was covering someone."

Except that she couldn't be covering anyone. She was just telling the truth, as always, that truth which, in the scales of justice, counts for nothing against a good alibi.

I hung up. I stayed sitting by the coffeepot and the phone, and started to think about this alibi. Let's analyse the situation. Who could he be? Don't reason, just think. Forget logic and think through love in love's terms. This character had so thoroughly transformed Thérèse that he could hardly have escaped unscathed himself. That night must have done something for him, too. Let's travel back through time, imagine Julie in Thérèse's shoes and Malaussène in the alibi's. Because my first real night with Julie was one hell of a renaissance, too! A Quattrocento for the body and soul. As soon as I woke up, I grabbed the phone and we started all over. That's right, telephone sex! Any technique can be used during a renaissance. Suppose the alibi knew nothing about Thérèse being arrested, why hadn't he phoned her? If Thérèse had given herself wholly to him, had she forgotten to tag on her address and phone number? Answer: no. Conclusion: he had called. Cold sweat. That morning, he'd called an empty hardware shop. He'd called while Clara was taking the kids to Passion Fruit, while Julie was investigating, while Half Pint and Jeremy were cultivating themselves at school and while I was bullying Theo. No doubt about it. The alibi had phoned. I could hear his eight rings as though the hardware shop was still echoing with them. Of course he'd phoned! He didn't know Thérèse was behind bars, and he'd called because he was dying to get at it again, by phone if need be. And if he had phoned, then he'd phone again. And soon.

I started staring at the phone until it became immaterial under the force of my gaze. Then I said to myself that if Thérèse had given her address to this character, then he could easily show up at any minute, that the door was going to burst open, that he was going to rush in and then instinctively leap into his lover's bed.

I didn't take my eyes off the door for the next two hours.

When it finally opened, I jumped to my feet.

It was the first time in my life that seeing Julie arrive was a disappointment.

She raised her eyebrows.

"What's up? Any news?"

I flopped down again. No, there was nothing new.

"What about you?"

Nor her. Julie had nosed round the politicos seen during the wedding clip. She'd come across two senators who were so shrivelled that not the slightest renaissance could be hoped for there, and a former minister who listened in to plenty of other people's phone calls, but had never confided anything private during his own. They were suitably saddened at the death of their colleague Roberval, and if they had any interest in his lady wife, then it was because she was the prime suspect. A fortune teller . . . Anything could be expected from such an interloper.

Julie had then gone round the film crew. Maybe Thérèse had become smitten during the excitement of the shoot. Nothing doing there, either. Just the charming smile of a cameraman ("a real hunk with it") who said that he was ready to do a remake of the wedding, with Julie in the starry dress and him in the tuxedo.

A hint of gratitude hung in Julie's voice. She is not one to neglect compliments. This was all I needed to put me at the top of the world. Julie must have noticed, because she asked:

"What's the matter, Benjamin? Something wrong?"

Her voice was a warm breeze sprinkling sand on my skin.

"Benjamin, Benjamin, if I had to screw every man alive, I'd choose you to stand in for all of them."

Which she promptly set about demonstrating by slipping beneath my pullover. It was time for the rematch. Theo, Hervé and the others could go back into training, their records were about to be shattered.

We were warming up nicely when the doorbell rang.

"Shit."

Yes, but given the circumstances, we could hardly refuse to open it.

It was little Leila, the last born of the Ben Tayebs.

"What's the matter, Ben? Are you hot?"

I sometimes wonder why I have this reputation for loving children.

"It's Hadouch," Leila went on. "He says you've got to come right away. He says he's got a surprise for you."

Chapter 18

I took the girl by the hand and we left Julie on duty at the hardware shop. The plain clothes coppers folded their newspapers and Belleville started following the parade again.

"It's at grand-dad's," Leila explained, while chasing the pigeons. "It's in the cellar."

I've always had mixed feelings about invitations to the Koutoubias' cellar.

"Good evening, my son, how are you?"

Old Amar was wiping up behind his bar.

"Fine, Amar, and how are things with you?"

He smiled at me through the fumes from the hookahs.

"Fine, thanks be to Allah, my son."

Stay for as long as possible on the surface. The Koutoubias' cellar was a lair of dark truths.

"And how's Yasmina?"

Dominoes were clacking on the tables. The air smelt of honey and aniseed.

"Fine, my son. Her blessings go to you."

Then, as I was about to open my mouth again:

"It's in the cellar."

I shut it. I nodded. Amar was right. This was an emergency. I went behind the bar. He opened the trapdoor and I dived down into the truth.

I can now affirm that the truth is featureless. At least, the version of it that Hadouch had to offer that day, curled up between the crates of bottles, lying on the shards of glass, was not a pretty sight.

"Don't worry, Ben, we've left him enough teeth so he can make his statement, and enough fingers so he can sign it."

Jesus Christ . . .

I just had enough strength to ask:

"Who is he?"

Hadouch, Mo and Simon looked tired. Their pickaxe handles weighed heavily in their hands.

"A tough nut."

"We had to crack his shell a bit."

"It took us all night, but we finally cracked him."

Who was it, for Christ's sake?

Simon squatted down:

"Tell Benjamin who you are, where you're from, and what you did."

Simon was smiling, with that gap between his incisors – the teeth of the Prophet – that always gave him an innocent air.

"Tell him everything, OK?"

The truth nodded what was presumably his head.

"Don't forget anything, now. We'll be listening, too. What's your name?"

Lips like inner tubes produced a chaplet of pink bubbles, but I couldn't make out what they were saying.

"Zhao Bang," Black Mo interpreted.

"Thérèse's Cantonese head-hunter," Hadouch confirmed. "Marie-Colbert's henchman. Or Ziba's husband, if you prefer. The servant in love. Zhao Bang and Ziba, the Tristan and Iseult of the *I Ching*, follow me?"

I followed him.

"We found him playing Mah-Jong in the backroom. He was gambling big money."

"With dollars."

"And where did these dollars come from?" Simon politely asked Zhao Bang. "Tell Benjamin where you got your dollars."

The inner tubes started gurgling again.

"From Roberval," Simon interpreted.

"And why did he pay you?"

For whacking Thérèse. It all fitted in with what Gervaise had told us. Marie-Colbert had got Zhao Bang to recruit Thérèse, then to eliminate her when the time was ripe. Zhao Bang had decided on a spot of arson. He just had to booby-trap the caravan. People would think a bottle of gas had exploded. An accident. But there'd been a cock-up. When he saw Thérèse go into her sanctuary, Zhao Bang had run to fetch Ziba his wife, so that she could deliver the bomb in a basket of rice. But Thérèse had left with her bag and the caravan was empty by the time Ziba arrived.

"You didn't know that the caravan was empty, did you?"

Zhao Bang shook his head. He thought Thérèse was still inside.

"And you set off the bomb from where you were standing?"

Yes, he'd had a remote control for that.

"In fact, you'd decided to kill two birds with one stone."

In fact, yes, that had been Zhao Bang's plan. To kill Thérèse contractually and murder Ziba from spite. His wife really had made Zhao Bang jealous. Ziba was driving him nuts. That much had been true from the word go.

"A human feeling," Hadouch remarked.

"And in this case the feeling was being done by a man from the post office," Mo explained. "Zhao suspected his wife of shagging a postman from Ramponneau. Isn't that right, Zhao?"

Zhao confirmed that it was.

Silence.

Good, so one problem solved. Thérèse had been cleared of blowing up her caravan and the victim had been identified. Not bad for a start.

The murmur from the Koutoubia could be heard through the intercom. Hadouch always remained plugged into the surface. You could clearly hear the domino players arguing and the customers' orders.

"And a merguez couscous!" Old Sole's voice yelped.

"Just like in a theatre," Hadouch grinned. "The wings listening to the stalls. It's the Comédie-Française here."

But there was still Marie-Colbert's murder. Given the state of the interviewee, I almost didn't want to ask. And yet, things having gone so far already, I ended up thinking out loud:

"And what about Marie-Colbert? Zhao didn't . . ."

Hadouch finished my question:

"Snuff Marie-Colbert? Zhao Bang? So he could split with the dosh, for instance? That's the first thing we asked him, of course. We've also been working for ourselves here. This isn't all pure charity. And no, it wasn't him. We were very insistent on that point. But it wasn't him. Was it, Zhao Bang?"

Zhao Bang shook his head.

"See?"

Black Mo then added:

"But it was him who hanged the other Roberval."

Sorry?

Simon, still squatting, asked:

"Remember Charles-Henri, Zhao? It was you who . . ."

Gesture.

Yes, another contract from Marie-Colbert. And another chapter for Julie's monograph. Charles-Henri had uncovered Marie-Colbert's gun-smuggling ring. Charles-Henri had been against the idea. Charles-Henri had threatened to reveal the whole set-up to the proper authorities. Charles-Henri de Roberval wanted to break with tradition, clean up the family name, bleach their coat of arms and be the first respectable Roberval. Oh, no humanitarian, just an honest politician. Everyone had to start somewhere. Charles-Henri had always been an eccentric, with a true sense of public property. The first in the entire dynasty. A black sheep, in fact. Marie-Colbert had felt hurt. Such behaviour could hardly be tolerated.

Silence again.

That disappointment that nearly always follows the revelation of the truth . . . Our curiosity is so easily satisfied, and our motives so samey: such is the dullness of crime. I looked at Zhao Bang. How many blokes would I have to put into a state like that before I found out who Thérèse had slept with? The truth was definitely beyond my means.

"By the way, any news of Thérèse's alibi?"

I shook my head.

"Want us to deal with that?" asked Mo, uncorking a bottle of Sidi Brahim.

The quest for truth is thirsty work. All I now had to do was give them the green light, and they'd turn Thérèse's demon lover into mince. I declined the offer.

"As you like."

"We're only trying to help."

The bottle was passed round. Upstairs, someone had put a coin in the jukebox, which broke into a long wail. An invisible veil fell over the cellar. It was the voice of Umm Kulthum. No customer could remember ever having heard anything else in the Koutoubia.

"When did she die again?" Mo asked.

"In '75," Simon answered.

"She'll be alive as long as my father keeps his bar open," Hadouch said.

"Tradition," Simon murmured.

"The Star of the Orient . . ."

They were on the point of breaking into tears when Zhao Bang spat out another chaplet of gurgles.

"What's he saying?"

"Nothing. He's just calling us filthy Arabs."

Zhao Bang was soon choking on his blood clots. Simon slapped him on the back and everyone went back to their meditations. Hadouch had never had the same aims in life as me. Right now, he was on a treasure hunt, while all I wanted was to get Thérèse out of the can. We sometimes used to discuss our differences. 'You're wrong about me, Benjamin. You think I'm a nice bloke because you're my friend and we went as far as S Levels together . . . Do you accord endless credit to Arabs and eggheads, Ben? Why not to the Swiss, garage mechanics and investigating magistrates? You're sentimental, my brother. Watch out, that's a fatal disease."

145

I glanced down at Zhao Bang's body. His breathing had become fairly regular again. I definitely did not like that cellar. I finally asked:

"What are you going to do with him?"

"He's going straight from the producer to the consumer," Hadouch replied.

He grabbed his pickaxe handle and hit the heavens three times. The heavens opened.

Archangels Titus and Silistri came down among us. They were alone. No Deputy Public Prosecutor Jual this time.

While they were taking Zhao Bang away, Police Lieutenant Silistri said:

"Jesus, don't these gamblers lay into each other something rotten!"

Before the heavens closed behind them, Titus added in an off-hand tone:

"By the way, Malaussène, you can go home. Your sister's been released. Her alibi finally showed up."

I obviously rushed upstairs, but Silistri stopped me halfway.

"Listen, Malaussène . . ."

The coppers exchanged glances.

"We'd like to prepare you for a shock . . ."

Titus then added:

"About the alibi . . ."

Silistri tried to take the plunge:

"I dunno what you'll make of it, but Titus and me talked it over, and we reckon that if she was our sister . . ."

But the water was obviously too cold.

So it was Titus who finally leapt in:

"We'd almost have preferred her to stay inside."

IX

The Saint Thérèse Passion

Chapter 19

"THEY'RE UPSTAIRS," JEREMY said when I burst through the front door of the hardware shop.

I leapt up the stairs but didn't find anyone in our bedroom. No-one, that is, apart from the usual company: Thérèse, Julie, Theo – plus Hervé who had apparently decided he could tag along too. No trace of the alibi. Where had they stashed the alibi? Were they really scared I'd ring Thérèse's alibi's neck?

When Theo got to his feet to adopt the role of defence attorney, I didn't beat about the bush:

"Shut it, you. We're going to put the nice uncle act on the back burner and let big bro listen to his little sis. You've already done enough damage as it is. You're disqualified, Theo. So belt up and let Thérèse have her say."

Julie took me seriously:

"Benjamin's right, Theo. Thérèse doesn't need anyone to defend her. She'll be fine on her own."

"Too right!" Thérèse said, with a defiant gleam in her eyes. "Hello, Benjamin, how are things? I did tell you not to worry about me ..."

It's always the same old story. A kid runs away from home,

you get into a terrible state, you imagine it's been flattened by a bus, horribly raped, sliced up into pieces and shoved into bin-liners, life itself is overwhelmed by a taste of death, and then the kid comes back. Upon which, what generally happens is that, instead of smothering it with kisses so it won't run away again, all you want to do is beat its brains out.

Thérèse seized both my hands, forced me to sit on the edge of the bed, crouched down in front of me and, like an English governess recruited for her patience, whispered:

"Calm down, calm down. I'm here now . . . I'll tell you the whole story."

Fine. So what was it exactly that I wanted to know? What she'd done that famous night? In the end, that was all I was interested in, wasn't it? Who really cared who killed Marie-Colbert? And who scarpered with the two suitcases full of dollars? Wasn't it pointless to ask where all that money made on the misery of the world had gone? The big question, the only one that mattered, was to know who Thérèse had slept with that night, wasn't it? Who was her famous alibi? And why had he made such a dread-ful impression on Inspectors Titus and Silistri?

"Is that it, Benjamin? Between tragedy and farce, you prefer the farce?"

Her stare forbade me to reply.

"All right, I'll tell you about my night of folly."

She was still holding my hands.

"But you'll have to wait for the punchline like everyone else. I'm going to tell you *everything*, right from the second I left the hardware shop up to the moment when I tiptoed back, imagining that you'd all be asleep. It was about three in the morning. It was pitch black. I didn't notice that the bedroom was empty. Mind you, if you had all been there, I don't think I'd have noticed that either. I was in a . . . strange state."

So there she was, back from her wedding. She woke up and crossed the hardware shop without looking at us. We kept her dinner warm in the oven, but she didn't touch it. She refused to meet the eyes that were following her. She was in no mood to talk. She was rigid with that stiffness she knew only too well. Sent back to the freezer of her adolescence.

"I'm going to put out Yemanja and pick up a few things."

And that's exactly what she was going to do. Draw the curtain on her old life, even though she hadn't started a new one. She felt so ashamed she wanted to die. As she walked down the road, it felt as though her bones were going to jut out through her skin. Luckily, it was dinner time and Belleville was practically deserted. She turned round two or three times to make sure Benjamin and Julius weren't following her. She slipped into her caravan without anyone noticing her. Her entire past lay in that tiny space. She put out Yemanja, cleared the shelves, tore down the curtains, stuffed her bits and bobs into one of those blue and white checked plastic bags that the Ben Tayebs use when they go back home on holiday. Her life was less full than the Ben Tayebs'. When the caravan was empty, her bag weighed almost nothing. She shut the door but didn't lock it. The caravan would make a good kip, or else could be taken over by a marabout. Once outside, she hesitated. She wanted to stash the contents of her bag in mum's tabernacle. In thirty years' time, someone would violate that wickerwork memory, as she had done, and also be amazed that the present had given no indication of the past.

But she couldn't go back to the hardware shop.

No hardware shop, no tribe, no explanations, no comfort, not yet. It was their discretion she feared more than anything else. That incubator silence, the way they had of letting a sorrow mature until it hatched out. Their patience as comforters, their indirect tenderness . . . No, she just couldn't bear that. What's more, they had the wrong idea about her. It was that other Thérèse who they'd try to comfort, their very own, the old Thérèse who never told a lie.

"But everything starts with a lie, Benjamin."

Yes, she'd lied to Benjamin. She'd finally freed herself of her big brother!

That was the only thing she didn't regret.

When Benjamin had sent along Rachida with the double astral data, Thérèse had immediately realised that it was about her and Marie-Colbert. But, for the previous few weeks, she'd preferred that man to the stars. A sudden turnabout in her values. This was the true loss of virginity and of her gift. She'd started to prefer love to the skies, five minutes with that man to the eternity of heaven. This new certitude meant that she was ready to defy the stars. It was simple. She'd just have to stop believing in them.

"Do you want to know the first thing that moved me about Marie-Colbert?"

It was his title. No, not exactly his title. More the way Marie-Colbert announced his title. *Councillor Grade One.* It reminded her of the Russian novels Benjamin used to read them when they were kids. There was all of Gogol in that title, 'Councillor Grade One', and all of Dostoyevsky, all of that Russian sadness seen in petty famished noblemen thinking that they exist by trotting out their titles. I'm a 'Councillor Grade One', quite something don't you think? Of course, Marie-Colbert didn't dwell on his title and was far from famished, but Christ, didn't he look like them, with his tall stiff body, and the childlike way he placed himself in his rank.

The fast-laner and the sorceress ... two lost souls ... that's what had moved her.

She listened to him, answered his questions, agreed to see him again, she was inwardly amused at his old school jargon, her heart ached at the tale of his terrible family, "he hid nothing from me about his family's crimes, absolutely nothing", so much so that she'd decided to give him a child at once and renew the blood line at last. She loved the idea of this marriage, and came up with excellent reasons for it – the wonderful couple of humanitarian smugglers – but the real truth of the matter was that during all that time her only thought had been for the moment when she'd undress Marie-Colbert, plunge that huge body into a steaming bath, slowly massage it, fill it with relaxation, then return that man to his real self. That had been her first thrill. The water of that bath had excited her. She felt as if her own stiffness would melt in it, that its heat would become hers. Then and only then would love become possible ...

"But, as you know, things didn't turn out quite like that."

Because of one small detail, perhaps: there had been *two* bathrooms in the Bahnhofstrasse suite.

"How to broach love after such a separation?"

When he slipped in between the sheets, Marie-Colbert performed his conjugal duties as though carrying out a contract. With no excessive enthusiasm. A condom. She hadn't got a word out of him since the signing session with Altmayer. Not a word. Not a caress. As for the hot bath, she had one alone. Afterwards. To soothe that dry burning in the midst of her body. And after

153

the water had gone completely cold around her, it was a block of ice and shame that had taken the night train home.

"Not a word of comfort, Benjamin! Just listen to the rest. So there I was, standing outside the caravan and once again refusing to be comforted."

Where could I go? Who could I see? Louna? That was one solution. If Laurent was off gallivanting, then Louna's misery would have distracted Thérèse from her own. The inconsolable Thérèse would have been the comforter. Things would go back to normal, in fact. But Thérèse had had no desire to console anyone. Thérèse was pissed off with the entire world. Above all with herself. With her own ridiculous ideas. For instance, all that crap about the bath! Months of dreaming about that bath when she'd now found out that baths and love don't mix. Water can only dehydrate love. This was an objective fact. Youngsters in love should never wash. Make love in the heat of your melting desire. Forget the preliminary bath. And don't wash afterwards, either. Keep it with you as long as you can.

"That gave me a real fit of the giggles."

Yes, sitting on the métro that was speeding her towards Paris, her plastic bag at her feet, a couple of slightly worried-looking lovers sitting opposite her, she was suddenly in the grip of that hysterical laughter which can at any moment degenerate into tears or fury. Fury, more like. She now knew where she was going. Back to Marie-Colbert! When he'd found her gone the next morning, he must have headed home, too. Why hadn't he contacted her? Why hadn't he phoned? Why hadn't he come to her? Didn't he realise that there's always a message in a woman's departure? So why hadn't he answered it? But asking too many questions exposes us to the answers. Because I'm useless, that's why! Because I'm nothing but a silly bitch! Because what I wanted was a bath more than a man, that's why! Because I was as cold and silent as the grave when he got into bed, that's why! Because I read *Woman, the Doctor of the House* too much and prepared myself for the combat of love like a pre-war Zurich woman! Because he didn't know how to go about it any more than I did, and God knows I didn't help him! But I loved him! I really loved him! I loved him and still do love him! I love him and am running to him! I'm running to him and this time I'll surrender myself to him! I'm running to him and this time he'll surrender himself to me! Stuff pride! Don't hold yourself back! The dam has burst! I'm flooding towards him!

She was no longer in the métro. She was running towards 60, Rue Quincampoix. I'll take him, take him over, snatch us from our pasts, our families, our fears. I'll make our bodies do the talking, I'll mingle us together for good, I'll plunge us into a night of love such as love has never seen before! No bath! No hesitation! No messing! Straight to the point! Pure invention! Everything is to be invented! Invent it from scratch and make a baby Roberval while we're at it! Strengthen the bloodline once and for all!

"That's just how I felt, Benjamin! I ran up his staircase and, how can I put it? I felt like I was diving into love!"

Silence in our bedroom. Julie, Theo, Hervé, all silent.
Me too.
And Thérèse out of breath.
As though just thinking about that night took her breath away.
Thérèse in love.
Her eyes sparkled, her hands were crushing mine.
So that was it?

That night, Thérèse de Roberval had quite simply made love with her husband . . .

A husband who'd just sent out a hitman . . .

Love reinvented, while the caravan was in flames . . .

Oh Titus . . . Oh Silistri . . . I see . . . I'm with you now . . . I get it . . . I understand . . . How right you were.

So, silence.

Immobility and silence.

Reinvented love . . . Then, a radiant Thérèse on her way back to the hardware shop, while someone was murdering her reinvented husband.

. . .

Until Thérèse's voice started up again, as deep as it could get: "You want to hear the rest, Benjamin?"

We could hardly stop now . . .

"Well, this time too, things didn't turn out quite as I'd expected."

No?

No.

He was waiting for her at the top of the staircase.

"Do you know what he said to me?"

Beaming with joy, she leapt up the last flight of stairs. When she turned on to the landing, she saw him, standing there in his suit, motionless. He was a bit pale, and in his stockinged feet. God knows why, but that was the first thing that struck her. Not his pallor, his socks. She still knew nothing about love, but her intuition whispered to her that certain pairs of socks kill desire more surely than the coldest of baths. So there he was, standing in his socks. He didn't smile. He didn't open his arms. He didn't welcome her. He just stared at that blue and white checked plastic bag and asked:

"Are you emigrating?"

Such irony in his voice . . . Everything that had been melting in her fossilised so rapidly that ice seemed to grip her heart. One of those shocks that can be lethal.

"What are you doing here?"

She was half dead when she replied. When she apologised. Tried to explain why she'd left Zurich. Why she'd run away. He cut her off:

"You didn't run away, Thérèse. You insulted me."

Not at all. It had been pure panic. Despair. She was sorry. She was back. Here she was. Here I am. I'm back. Against his icy delivery, she stuck with her ardent tone. Everything was still possible.

"It's too late now."

He turned his back on her, went into his apartment and pulled at the door which she was frantically trying to keep open. He hesitated, shrugged, then let her in. By the door, she noticed the two suitcases with metal corners that Altmayer had given them, Marie-Colbert's coat waiting on the back of a chair, the pair of shoes he'd been about to put on when she rang the bell, and which he was now carefully lacing while talking to her about Madame Bovary. Yes, while lecturing her about Emma Bovary. While telling Thérèse that she was a sort of Bovary. He added:

"But without the curves."

Then he smiled.

"You don't believe in the stars any more, Thérèse?"

His question caught her unawares.

"Nor in the tarot?"

He'd just laced his second shoe.

"Take my word for it, you ought to have a reading done."

He looked up at her, his hands on his knees.

"It would tell you of the inevitable other woman."

What?

"My sister-in-law. Charles-Henri's widow."

He added:

"When I am deserted, I bounce back at once."

She tried to protest. She tried to tell him that she hadn't deserted him. He stopped her by uttering the longest sentence of their entire conversation:

"It doesn't matter, Thérèse, you and I were a mistake, not only must the Robervals avoid misalliances, but they should marry only amongst themselves."

With his laces tied, he was now on his feet. He went to get his coat.

"That is precisely what I am going to do. As soon as we are divorced."

He produced an envelope from his inside pocket.

"I shall marry my sister-in-law, Charles-Henri's widow."

He showed her a plane ticket and concluded:

"Excuse me now. I was on my way out. I am going to join her."

Jesus, Thérèse . . .

"Just don't say a word, Benjamin. I repeat, I don't need to be comforted."

Which she then proved at once.

"Do you know what his sister-in-law's name is?"

With the cheeky smile of someone about to come out with a good one.

"Zibeline!"

Then, in a fit of merry cynicism:

"A first name like that implies a big spender. Marie-Colbert was the man for her. But now the poor thing's been widowed all over again."

The idea that Zibeline had gone off alone with Altmayer's suitcases after chucking her second husband over the banisters was now burning in Julie's eyes. But why was the corpse in its stockinged feet when Marie-Colbert had just laced up his shoes? And why had the stiff looked so merry? And who was the alibi?

Thérèse let go of my hands. She needed them to belittle her rival's charms, "a sort of big blob of make-up, you know the sort". Her fingers were fluttering around. She just couldn't understand "how anybody could . . ."

"Thérèse, what did you do during the rest of the night?"

She stopped, her mouth agape. She slapped her thigh.

"Silly me. The alibi question! I'd completely forgotten!"

Go ahead, I thought, take the piss. But I'm not budging till I know.

"The alibi . . . the alibi . . ." she chanted. "So where do you imagine I went after leaving Marie-Colbert, Benjamin?"

Chapter 20

"COME ON, TRY and guess. Where would I have wanted to go after leaving Marie-Colbert's house? Picture me there in the street, in tears, with my shopping bag, that door closed behind me forever. Where to go now? The hardware shop? No way. Louna? She'd only have made me even more depressed. So?"

All this pronounced with the jollity of a summer camp leader, as though we were supposed to find some trinket hidden in the dorm before lights out.

"You can do it, Benjamin. Make an effort. Put yourself in my shoes. Because," she added, "I did precisely what you would have done!"

I just didn't get it. All that panic had blindfolded me.

"Come on," Thérèse insisted. "When your life falls to pieces, when you're up to your neck in it, when Jeremy burns his school down, for example, or when you're being accused of bombing the Store, *who* do you go and see, Benjamin? And when you're wondering where your sister Thérèse spent the night, *who* do you go and ask?"

Jesus Christ . . .

"Ah, you're getting warm. You're nearly there. 3, Rue aux Ours is two hundred yards from Marie-Colbert's place . . ."

I stared round at Theo, who immediately went on the defensive:

"Hervé and I did try and tell you that she'd come to see us, Ben, but we couldn't get a word in edgeways. You told us to answer your questions yes or no, and when we tried to say anything else you went haywire."

"It was absolutely terrifying," Hervé confirmed.

"The only thing you didn't ask was whether Thérèse had come to see us. You burst in like a thing possessed then left like a rocket . . ."

Thérèse sweetly gestured with her hands.

"You see, Benjamin, I did what everyone in the family does when things go wrong. I went to see Theo."

"Stop!"

I bellowed "stop!", then tried to explain as calmly as possible that I didn't give a tuppenny toss about the intermediate stages. So, after leaving Marie-Colbert, Thérèse had gone to see Theo. Fine. I hadn't even given Theo the chance to tell me. Fair enough. Theo was the occasional refuge for our tribe when times were hard. How true. Theo was wonderful. Good old Theo. My hearty thanks to him. But what I now wanted to know was what Thérèse had done that night *after* having sobbed her eyes out on our priceless uncle Theo's shoulder.

"For Christ's sake, Thérèse, where the fuck did you spend the rest of the night? I warn you I'm starting to get stroppy. Where did you go afterwards?"

At which point all three of them started talking at the same time, Thérèse to tell me that there'd been no afterwards, that it had been the end of her treasure hunt for love, that she'd rushed round to Theo's place instead of chucking herself in the Seine, a broken woman even before she'd reached full womanhood, in a terrible state, Ben, Theo confirmed, more convinced than ever, the poor thing, Hervé chipped in, that she'd never love and never be loved, while we were up to our ears in love, Theo thoughtfully reminded me, and so they'd both welcomed her with open arms, with the same enthusiasm, warmed her with their heat, dried her tears, given her their bed, tucked in that tragically naked despair, with such tenderness, Thérèse added, such tenderness that they gradually returned her to that state of womanhood which her passion for Marie-Colbert had at least allowed her to glimpse, nothing had been lost, she started to think, the embers were still warm, with just the merest tinge of red, almost reduced to ashes perhaps, but still gleaming with a tiny spark, so they had blown on those embers, as I would have done if I'd been there and if Thérèse hadn't been my sister, it was not really their vocation, of course, but emergencies can transcend differences, they had been given a primordial mission not to let the last spark of humanity go out, and they certainly agreed with Thérèse when it came to the baby question, we tried to tell you about that too, Ben, but you just wouldn't listen, the vital question of babies – and here even the Pope would have been in agreement – and so it went from embers to a spark, from a spark to a merry blaze, and from a merry blaze to a towering inferno, the three of them had lit a conflagration which utterly engulfed them, a somewhat disconcerting conflagration at that, since all they'd been thinking about was Thérèse's future, for if Thérèse had got married it hadn't just been for a laugh, but with a view to the future, and the future always means a baby, and this baby, by the way, was not going to be born into the worst of families, it would be brought up by none other than Benjamin Malaussène, just think of it, how many other babies will envy its good fortune, would just love to make off with a dad like that, and once the vital question of upbringing had been dealt with, the three of them set about creating the future, the three of them merrily licked the future into shape, firstly as a needful consolation, but soon with unbridled desire, for a child's happiness is born at the moment when it is conceived, any paediatrics manual will tell you that, Benjamin, so there had been a joyous unleashing of good will, to such an extent that the other tenants in the building woke up in a puritanical fury, banging on all the walls and with the full force of their frustration, shouting that they were going to complain to all the proper authorities, as invariably happens when real life emerges, but they didn't care, they were the future in action, and not just that of Thérèse, they were the human race's sumptuous future . . .

Until Thérèse, who turned out to be highly gifted, by the way, infinitely inventive, as we can be when we give ourselves over body and soul to a worthwhile project, until Thérèse left them there, more dead than alive – in the state I'd found them in – completely drained of that life they'd filled her with, left them there panting and ran through the insults that rained from the windows towards a passing cab, "I wanted to be back before dawn, I was scared you'd tell me off, Benjamin", and now I'd heard it all, and if Thérèse had refused to spill the beans to Deputy Public Prosecutor Jual, then it had not been only to preserve Theo's honour, or that of Hervé, no, Thérèse had insisted on saving the honour of Homosexuality, with a capital H, no less, that's what she'd done, she was just marvellous!

Theo lisped.

"Sublime," Hervé confirmed. "Thérèse was sublime!"

The heights of enthusiasm.

From which Thérèse slowly returned to earth.

Talking of the sublime, and the sublime and a half, then Theo and Hervé were no slouches when it came to the sublime, and it was their heroics when they freed her from prison that must have made such a strong impression on Inspectors Titus and Silistri.

"Listen, Benjamin. Listen to what they did to get me released."

Nothing that extraordinary, according to Theo.

"When you'd gone, Ben, we drank your coffee and spent ten minutes under an ice-cold shower."

If they agreed with Thérèse that love was incompatible with water, they nevertheless recognised that warriors found a use for it. Sword blades were tempered in it to sharpen them. And they now realised that they'd have to sharpen their wits for the coming combat. They were about to assail a social fortress and, in the midst of that fortress, attack the keep itself, tear Thérèse from police headquarters, no less, situated in the justly infamous Conciergerie. So they were Thérèse's alibi. But who would believe them? What credence would they be given? They felt big enough to overcome the force's professional scepticism – after all, they were bearers of the truth – but not its prejudices. Nor its insistence on likelihood. No-one would believe them. Not them. They weren't the men for the job. They were supposed to have blissed out a woman? Never in a million years. This realisation worried them. It would mean that Thérèse would have no alibi. But the cold water tempered them. Deciding if it had first been Theo's idea or Hervé's would have set off a bitter-sweet debate which the urgency of their tale excluded. One of them had had *the idea*, that was all. Since they were not worthy of belief, then they'd have to come up with some reliable witnesses. That was the idea. Now, there were witnesses in plenty who'd spent the night banging on the walls, ceiling and floor. These witnesses had heard Thérèse's ascension at the moment when Marie-Colbert was taking a dive. Then the witnesses had seen Thérèse running across the tarmac while Marie-Colbert had been stretched out for hours on his ancestral marble. The witnesses all knew Theo well and so scorned him for his sexual proclivities, and were now getting to know Hervé, too, who "was no better than the other one" . . . Ideal witnesses! Ear witnesses as much as eye witnesses! Even nose witnesses, if need be! But more than anything else, they were reliable witnesses, gold-plated respectable citizens, guardians of order, who the police would believe as soon as they set their eyes on them, for they were the eyes of the police. They would quite simply have to be talked into carrying out their threats. Persuaded to go and complain . . . This had been the trickiest part of the scheme.

"I even had to pay one of them to complain."

"Really!" Hervé sighed.

The plan finally gelled. A vociferous hoard followed them to police headquarters on Quai des Orfèvres. A whole apartment block of alibis! Statements and signatures! Nocturnal antics, Deputy Public Prosecutor, sir! Complaints and affidavits galore! Disgusting! Our children heard it all! Such a din! Impossible to sleep! Work the next day! The honour of the small tradesman! Bribed or volunteers, they formed a moral guild determined to make its point. And twice, not just once! We won't let the matter drop! They pushed Theo and Hervé down Deputy Public Prosecutor Jual's corridor, as though they had made the arrest themselves, so overexcited that Inspectors Titus and Silistri had feared for Thérèse's life.

"On my mother's life, Malaussène", Titus later confirmed during his own version of the events. "When we saw Thérèse's two archangels arrive with that mob of crazed virtue at their heels, we were scared for her."

"We even wondered if she wouldn't be safer in custody," Silistri admitted.

Deputy Public Prosecutor Jual had had the opposite reaction. He did the necessary, then opened the doors of freedom for Thérèse. After having officially admonished the three delinquents, he whispered in Hervé's ear as he passed by:

"Wonderful. Keep it up."

"He's not bad at all, your Deputy Public Prosecutor Jual," Theo concluded. "He let Thérèse go with all the honours she deserved."

"Not bad, and not a bad looker," Hervé confirmed.

Julie and I were too drained to comment. We left the three of them upstairs. We even gave them our room for the night. Thérèse wanted to introduce the two fathers of her child to the entire tribe the next morning, "to make things quite clear, and so there'll be no misunderstanding".

Then Julius the Dog scratched at the door. It was time for Martin Lejoli.

X

In which we come to the inevitable epilogue

Chapter 21

NINE MONTHS LATER – and for the first time in my long experience in this field – I saw a baby emerge from its mother's womb, then look right and then left. It was a girl. With Papa Theo on one side and Papa Hervé on the other, Mother Thérèse on her white bed, her first expression was of satisfaction ... Then her little forehead crinkled as she did her sums. A third candidate, standing behind Hervé, looked just as moved as the other two. Had she noticed that the third candidate was stroking Papa Hervé's palm with the back of his hand? Had she noticed that, on the other side of the bed, Papa Theo was disapproving of Deputy Public Prosecutor Jual's gesture? Whatever the case, when the new arrival's eyes finally came to rest on me I could see in them her deep understanding of the world's complexity, and a burning desire for someone to give her a user's manual.

"It looks like she's chosen you, Benjamin," declared Thérèse and handed her to me.

That was one way to interpret her SOS. Her downy head exactly fitted into the palm of my hand. It was boiling with the desire to understand.

"You're going to play the part of the one and only father," Theo confirmed. "It was with that in mind that we conceived her, in fact," he added, not taking his eyes off Hervé and Deputy Public Prosecutor Jual.

Clara's flash certified my appointment. The baby didn't even blink. Her stare was holding on to my mine like an anchor. Another one whose embrace would not desert me for quite some time.

"Blame your charisma, Malaussène," Julie whispered, when she saw the expression on my face.

I stared back at little thingummy. "Years of attentive upbringing, and when you want to do a runner, you'll go and ask Papa Theo's permission, is that it?"

"What ardour in her eyes," Gervaise exclaimed. "This one is a real passion fruit!"

Jeremy, who'd been silently pensive up until then, immediately declared:

"And that's what we're going to call her."

Instead of grimacing and resisting, as Thérèse usually did each time Jeremy baptised, she treated us to her new laughter:

"Passion Fruit? You want to call my daughter Passion Fruit Malaussène, with capitals everywhere so she'll end up going to the School of Schools like Marie-Colbert? No way! You can do better than that."

"Maracuja," said Jeremy.

Thérèse's laughter stopped as she savoured the word.

"Maracuja . . ."

"It's what the Brazilians call the passion fruit," Jeremy explained.

"Maracuja," chanted Half Pint. "Maracuja . . . Maracuuuuuu-uja . . . "

Who thus made her triumphal entry into the tribe under the name Maracuja Malaussène.

Chapter 22

WE CELEBRATED MARACUJA'S arrival that very evening with an extravagant méchoui at the Koutoubia, naturally. Rachida's little Ophélie had popped out three days before and Old Amar had decided to mark both events with a huge combined do. Since Gervaise was there, our first parental act was to sign up the two future little women at Passion Fruit. The holy mother made no objection, but her playgroup was in difficulty now that the local authority was not going to renew her grant. Officially, there was talk of "other priorities", but Gervaise knew that the decision had been made under an avalanche of petitions. Her whorelets were a black mark on the neighbourhood. (And never forget, Maracuja, black marks are never priorities.)

"Malaussène, if you need any help bringing up Maracuja," Inspector Titus remarked after seeing the worried look on my face. "Then we can provide you with an entire building of morally irreproachable godfathers and godmothers."

"We can even hand her over to them straightaway, if you want."

Apparently, they found that highly amusing. Hadouch, Mo and Simon joined in the laughter. This was a tetchy matter too, Maracuja, this temporary alliance between the police and the thieves. But that's humanity for you, isn't it? There's no hope of reform . . .

"Your job is to catch murderers," I grumbled snidely.

"He's referring to our dearly departed Marie-Colbert," said Titus to Silistri.

"He's criticising our slow progress," Silistri remarked.

"It sounds like he's almost disappointed he isn't inside," Hadouch observed.

"Put yourself in his shoes," Jeremy concluded. "He bent our ears for months about that crap."

Have you made the right choice, Maracuja? You've picked a minority father.

Titus started into an explanation:

"We did think of running you in, Malaussène, but there was too much competition this time. Who do you reckon had it in for Roberval even more than you, and made off with his dosh?"

Silistri summed up nine months of inquiries:

"Just by looking through his customers we found a nice list of suspects: the Irish of Ireland, the Armenians of Armenia, the Chiapas of Mexico, the Peruvians of the *Sendero Luminoso*, the Sahrawis of Polisario, the Corsicans just about everywhere, the Basques, Kosovars, Uzbeks, Palestinians, Kurds, Ugandans, Cambodians, Congolese . . ."

"To which you can add all the more or less secret services which Roberval armed against them at the same time . . . Sorry, Malaussène, this time there were far too many on the list ahead of you. We had to drop you as a lead."

"And the result?"

"The result is that we stand about as much chance catching the killer as you do of stopping Maracuja from falling in love one day."

The fact is, Maracuja, the fact is . . .

We'd reached this point in our pre-dinner chat, the main course of the méchoui not having been served yet, when Old Sole put in a rowdy appearance, chanting:

"Sidi-Brahim all round!"

Hadouch, Mo and Simon turned round in unison.

"It's your round, is it Sole?"

This was an unheard-of event in the history of the Koutoubia.

"A round for everyone, then wine with the dinner!" Old Sole confirmed. "Sidi-Brahim for all the families concerned."

"Have you come into some money?" Simon asked.

Sole's usual diet was a quarter litre of red wine with a plain merguez couscous. Coming from him, there was something decidedly fishy about this round.

"Long live births!" Sole barked back, clearly not waiting for his first glass of the evening.

What happened next was rapid and discreet. Hadouch bent over Jeremy's ear, who silently nodded his head, stood up, took Half Pint, Leila and Nourdine with him, then, as he passed in front of Titus and Silistri:

"Oi, the boys in blue, come and give us a hand. Old Sole's treating us all, and we need a relay team for the Sidi-Brahim. You in the cellar, us on the ladder, Nourdine and Leila in the bar. We'll need a good sixty bottles, OK?"

When the policemen had vanished down into the cellar, Hadouch motioned to Mo to sit down beside Sole, who had himself chosen a chair near Simon.

Sole looked first at Mo, then at Simon, who were now either side of him. His grin grew broader.

"All right?"

174

Mo and Simon assured him that they were all right.

From the moment Sole had turned up, something had frozen in Hadouch's eyes. The old man's external appearance had scarcely changed, his suit still looked like an overgrown wasteland, but internally Sole looked more poised. The master of the universe. He was smiling.

And offering drinks all round.

Motioning to me to stay put, Hadouch slid his chair over to face the new arrival.

"Sorry, I didn't mean to kick you."

"It doesn't matter," Sole assured him.

But, as he apologised, Hadouch bent down and looked under the table. He whistled in admiration.

"Well, well, well, what lovely new shoes we've got!"

"They're old ones," Sole answered after a slight hesitation.

"They don't look old," Hadouch remarked while sitting back up, one of Sole's shoes in his hand.

"Give me my shoe back!" Sole yelled.

Mo and Simon were holding him down on the bench.

Hadouch put the shoe down on the table.

"Benjamin, does this look like an old shoe to you?"

It was spanking new. With the profile of a luxury steamer.

"I made them ages ago!" Sole shouted. "To measure! Then I kept them. They're my last pair. Crocodile skin. Hand made in the 1930s. Come on, give it me back!"

Hadouch smiled sweetly.

"Were you English when you were young, Sole?"

The old man started.

"No, of course not, why?"

"Cos these are English shoes. Look, it says so inside."

He handed him the evidence.

"A grand each," Simon said.

"Two grand for the pair," Mo confirmed.

"At the very least," Hadouch murmured.

Everyone fell silent. But no-one dared to believe what seemed to have been revealed in that silence haunted by a ghost in its stockinged feet.

"I didn't kill him," Sole mumbled. "I swear, it wasn't me!"

The first bottles had reached the tables.

"Sole, hurry up and tell us before Titus and Silistri come back up from the cellar . . ."

Chapter 23

OLD SOLE HADN'T killed Marie-Colbert de Roberval. Not exactly. But who would have believed his story if he'd told it to the cops? Sole had felt sorry for Thérèse, but if he'd come forward, then he'd have been sent down for life. Sole knew what the boys in blue were like. They didn't believe in miracles. So what's your story, Sole? We believe in miracles, we do. Come on, spill the beans. Tell us why old Roberval gave you his shoes! As a thank-you present? No, Marie-Colbert hadn't given him his shoes. Did you nick them, then? No, not exactly. What then? It was silly, really. Sole had been very very silly to go and see Marie-Colbert at his house.

"How's that?"

"You went to his place?"

"That very night?"

That very night, at that very time, at that very address, 60 Rue Quincampoix, at his town house. How daft of him. Sole knew the place, because he'd been there once, when Thérèse had introduced him as one of her witnesses for the wedding. He'd found Marie-Colbert very nice, very simple, no 'Monsieur', call me Marie-Colbert. So Sole had reckoned that it was do-able.

"Do-able, what was do-able?"

The idea he was going to suggest. What idea for crying out loud? Stop beating about the bush! You want to send us to sleep, or what? You want us to go and fetch Titus and Silistri? But it was really stupid of me, like I told you. So stupid you'd never understand! We're all as thick as shit, too, Sole! Except for Hadouch and Benjamin who had a higher education. The rest of us are all shitheads. We'll understand.

"OK."

So, this was Old Sole's idea. This was the idea my old noddle came up with. We respect the aged, Sole, go on, never fear, tell us all.

"I did tell you, Benjamin, that Thérèse's loss of her gift after her marriage was bad news for me."

It certainly was bad news for him, since while Thérèse was still clairvoyant she sorted out the little future Sole had left. Come what may, she picked the first three horses in a race for him once a week, usually in the wrong order, but this still made him an average of two thousand francs per week. Or eight thousand per month. The loss of her gift meant a drastic drop in Sole's income.

"So, I thought Marie-Colbert might be able to step in."

"To step in what?"

"I thought he might be able to make up for what I'd lost. What does two thousand francs a week mean to someone like Marie-Colbert?"

"Stop! You're not going to tell us you went round there to claim . . ."

"I did tell you it was a daft idea."

All the same, Marie-Colbert had seen him. After Thérèse's

visit, Marie-Colbert had had to put off his departure to the airport and had summoned Zhao Bang to report on his failed hit. The doorbell rang, Marie-Colbert confidently opened it, but instead of Zhao Bang (who later told Hadouch, Mo and Simon that he broke his appointment), there was Old Sole. Sole clambered up to see Marie-Colbert, who furiously listened to him on the landing. But what could he do? He was on the point of leaving, with two suitcases at his feet, he was expecting a hitman and this old fool had shown up. So Marie-Colbert listened to him (with his rounded butt perched on the cast-iron banister rail). And when Sole stated his request – a pension of two thousand francs a week, or eight thousand a month – his host just couldn't believe his ears. Given the circumstances, he found it so funny that he burst out laughing, his arse on the banister rail and, instead of rolling in the aisles, rolled over backwards to laugh himself quite literally to death four floors down. He was out of practice. He didn't laugh very often. And that killing joke remained frozen on his face even in death.

"I saw him fall, I tried to save him. His shoes came off in my hands. That's all."

Silence. One hell of a silence. On the jukebox even Umm Kulthum had taken five. Then Hadouch leant right down over Sole. He whispered:

"What about the cases?"

" . . . "

" . . . "

"In all honesty, I just couldn't leave them there. Someone might have stolen them."

"Where are they?"

" . . . "

"..."

"..."

"At home."

By the time I'd caught on to what Sole had said, Mo and Simon had vanished. Hadouch was smiling.

"Don't worry, Sole, we won't tell Titus and Silistri. In exchange for our silence, we're going to look after your capital. We'll pay your pension. I'll even give you a raise. Two thousand five hundred a week. How does that sound?"

"Three thousand," said Sole.

"Two thousand six hundred," Hadouch suggested.

"Eight," Sole insisted.

"Seven . . ."

"We mustn't forget Passion Fruit," Gervaise butted in, even though she shouldn't have heard a word of this hushed conversation.

Hadouch froze. What calibre ears did this woman have?

"That's right," Gervaise went on. "We'll have to think of Ophélie and Maracuja."

Hadouch was cornered and Gervaise looked relieved.

"We'll be able to do without the council grant."

Hadouch nodded as vaguely as possible.

"And open up a few more playgroups," she remarked.

Hadouch raised a hand to stop her, but Gervaise was already shaking her head in compassion:

"There are so many whorelets in this terrible world!"

She looked worried again:

"Hadouch, do you think those suitcases contain enough money for all those kids?"

Hadouch opened his hands and his mouth . . .

"Once Sole's pension has been deducted, of course," Gervaise conceded.

The last bottles arrived on the tables. Titus and Silistri were going to resurface any moment.

"Unless we give it all to the police benevolent fund . . ." she suggested.

Hadouch's mouth was still opening and closing like a goldfish's gob in its bowl. There was despair in his eyes when he turned to me. But what did he expect me to do? You'll see, Maracuja, you can't win 'em all. Not even when you're uncle Hadouch.

"So we agree then, Hadouch," Gervaise concluded in a whisper. "It would be far better for all that money to go to Passion Fruit . . ."

Also by Daniel Pennac
in English translations by Ian Monk

THE FAIRY GUNMOTHER

Maybe the worst indignity for a Paris cop is to be shot dead by an old granny he is trying to help across the street in Paris on a frosty morning. She packs an ancient P38 of German manufacture – she must have a suspicious nature. Who gets pulled in as accessory to murder is that professional scape-goat, Benjamin Malaussène, whose life is already sufficiently complicated by the possession of an epileptic dog, Julius, and some dozen siblings, the result of his industrious mother's casual encounters. In this crowded household, which offers shelter to a number of elderly smack-heads who live for their dose of amphetamines, and for which Benjamin acts as proxy mother, peace and quiet are unknown – and Benjamin's voluptuous and too-enterprising girlfriend Julie would see to it remaining so if no-one else did. But those resourceful coppers, after arresting all the wrong people, eventually pick up a lead to smashing a sinister drug-ring: yes, the finger of guilt eventually points at . . . oh dear! Fancy that! . . .

"Daniel Pennac's Belleville novels, centring on a character called Malaussène, have apparently acquired cult status in France. It is easy to see why. He writes brightly, and, the translation by Ian Monk suggests, in a crisp demotic style"
                                        ALLAN MASSIE, *Scotsman*

"Already a bestseller in its native coutry, it deserves to be one here if there's any justice in the world of crime"   MAXIM JAKUBOWSKI, *Time Out*

"There is only profit and pleasure to be had in this wise, good-humoured, funny book"   DAVID COWARD, *TLS*

"An exceptionally enjoyable piece of French *noir* with plenty of humour and pathos thrown in"   *Liverpool Daily Post*

THE SCAPEGOAT

His title is Quality Controller, but Benjamin's function at The Store is scapegoat for the impatience, sometimes the rage, of the customers. So sweet is his nature, so eloquent his contrition, that most of the indignant and misused victims withdraw their complaints. But there is also the little matter of the bombs that keep exploding very close to where Benjamin is standing. Suspicion falls on him, even as he and his voluptuous mistress Julie have begun to unearth an even deeper mystery, a sinister and sordid conspiracy whose unravelling will expose yet one more seam in the dark heart behind the beguiling veneer of contemporary Paris.

"A charming, idiosyncratic tale"   MAX DAVIDSON, *Daily Telegraph*

"If you want to read something that's witty, inventive, shocking and great fun, pick up a Pennac"   PAUL DUNCAN, *Crime Time*

"Pennac is slick and funny, and Monk's translation brings over the fun of the French. Cartoon crime – very cool, very continental"   *Guardian*

"Loopily clever and entertaining thriller . . . Pennac's world is well worth entering. His plotting is enjoyably tricky, his sense of humour jaunty, his transitions roller-coasterishly abrupt. These are thrillers that make demands"
          DENNIS DRABELLE, *Washington Post*

WRITE TO KILL

Benjamin Malaussène is a downtrodden publisher at Vendetta Press. Treated as a scapegoat by Queen Zabo, the redoubtable doyenne of publishing, he has finally had enough. After one row too many with her, he resigns, only for Zabo to offer him a starring role. All he has to do is to impersonate the world's best-loved, but hitherto anonymous author, J. L. B. As always, however, things are never simple for Malaussène and his extended family of misfits and chancers. Soon, he is in it deep: the theft of a manuscript, a frenzied readership, his private life in disarray, and then a spate of connected murders which threaten to destroy Vendetta Press.

"Pennac is a cult in Paris . . . for the continuous burlesque provided by Malaussène's extended family of Belleville 'misfits and chancers'. There a good moments that remind of Heller and John ('Garp') Irving"

DIGBY DURRANT, *London Magazine*

"Pennac's tongue-in-cheek unrealism is fast-paced, stylish and hugely entertaining, a mixture of crime spoof and the stock-in-trade of fairy tale . . . Ian Monk, catching the jokes and matching the argot, has translated Pennac splendidly. In this intelligent, feel-good fiction, everyone has a good story to tell."

DAVID COWARD, *TLS*

"Pace, construction, sense of locale and wit all serve to keep the works [also *The Fairy Gunmother* and *The Scapegoat*] firmly to hand until finished and in mind once you've done so. Lovely covers too" OMER ALI, *Time Out*

"It is difficult to describe this author's unique and bizarre style, short of saying that it has all the earmarks of achieving the kind of cult success in other countries that it did in France" BARRY FORSHAW, *Crime Time*